CHASING REMBRANDT

by Richard Stevenson

A Donald Strachey Mystery
Book 17

Foreword by Zachary Lipez

ReQueered Tales
Los Angeles • Toronto
2023

CHASING REMBRANDT

by Richard Stevenson

A Donald Strachey Mystery, Book 17

First American edition: 2023

This edition: ReQueered Tales, May 2023

ReQueered Tales version 1.21
Kindle edition ASIN: B0C448YMV5
Paperback edition ISBN-13: 978-1-951092-93-1
Hardcover edition ISBN-13: 978-1-951092-94-8

For more information about current and future releases,
please contact us:
E-mail: *requeeredtales@gmail.com*
Facebook (Like us!): www.facebook.com/ReQueeredTales
Twitter: @ReQueered
Instagram: www.instagram.com/requeered
Web: www.ReQueeredTales.com
Blog: www.ReQueeredTales.com/blog
Mailing list (Subscribe for latest news): https://bit.ly/RQTJoin

Praise for
Donald Strachey series

"Stevenson has deftly picked up where he left off ... A tightly plotted, fast-paced, entertaining mystery full of twists and turns that will keep you guessing until the very end."

— Lambda Rising Book Report

"A warm welcome back to Donald Strachey – who's returned to us just in time to walk into a minefield of issues affecting our besieged and contentious community. This admirable, absorbing new mystery has all the immediacy and realism of a telegram from the front."

— Katherine V. Forrest

"Sassy and sexy ... Don Strachey is a private dick who really earns his title."

— Armistead Maupin

"Stevenson writes wittily and knowingly about his subjects, both the gay world and the world of politics, and draws telling portraits of the bitter, clever amusing men who inhabit both."

— West Coast Review of Books

"Strachey departs from the classic noir protagonist in two crucial respects. First, he's an openly gay man firmly embedded in Albany's late 70s gay scene. Second, he's funny and sane, not broody and neurotic – the anti-Philip Marlowe. The first aspect gives [this series] its historical and cultural value and the second is what makes it a pleasure, a joy, to read."

— Michael Nava

Also by RICHARD STEVENSON

THE DONALD STRACHEY NOVELS

Death Trick (1981)

On the Other Hand, Death (1984)

Ice Blues (1986)

Third Man Out (1992)

Shock to the System (1995)

Chain of Fools (1997)

Strachey's Folly (1998)

Tongue Tied (2003)

Death Vows (2008)

The 38 Million Dollar Smile (2009)

Cockeyed (2010)

Red, White and Black and Blue (2011)

The Last Thing I Saw (2012)

Why Stop at Vengeance (2015)

www.dropdead (2016)

Killer Reunion (2019)

Chasing Rembrandt (2023)

CHASING REMBRANDT

by Richard Stevenson

Table of Contents

FOREWORD

I hear my dad speaking on every page of *Chasing Rembrandt*, which sucks, as it's a pretty distant second choice to how I'd prefer to hear his voice. I hear my dad speaking when I write as well (and not just when I use "disinterested" when what I mean is "uninterested"). If this foreword feels a bit precious, it's because I write pretentiously to avoid being taken over by my father's voice. Even touching on a language that sounds like it might come out of a human person's mouth makes me hear my dad in my ear, gently imitating the patter of a Lockhaven cousin, a Dept of Education apparatchik from Addis Ababa, or the proprietor of the Otis Chicken Farm; every breathing-on-the-page soul given the same dignity other authors might only grant to protagonists. And if I attempt to imitate my father's voice, as it gently imitates others with an empathy I can only aspire to, I just end up talking to myself. Because an approximation is better than nothing; that pretty meager Plan B, compared to him still being alive, but what can you do? So, if this foreword seems, to the reader, to be written in a stylized manner that ill suits the light heart of the novel it's attached to, if the reader thinks maybe the book's author deserved better, I can only say; yeah, he did deserve better. He deserved to be writing this foreword himself, happily basking in some well-earned, late-career attention, writing on his yellow legal pad, in the dusty sunlight of his study, while waiting for his dear husband Joe to get back from the sculpting studio. My dad deserved that. Not this solipsistic sad-sackery telegraphing only an absence of joie de vivre, an absence antithetical to its subject's slapstick sensibilities, an absence of good cheer as glaring as the hole in the world my dad left when he fucked off for the mild green pastures of Presbyterian heaven. (Richard was agnostic, and not in any rush to graduate to whatever buttery paradise his Pennsylvanian ancestors subscribed to, but I do like to think of him existing somewhere.)

As an author, Richard Stevenson (Lipez, i.e. dad) revered the atmosphere and hard bop dread of Raymond Chandler and *Chinatown*. He admired both the bone dry (and darkly amusing) economy of *The Friends of Eddie Coyle*, and Bruce Chatwin's differently attentive rendering of local color. My dad took inspiration from the intricately plotted mousetraps of Karin Slaughter, inhabited as they were by lived-in protagonists. He enthusiastically admired the incisive world building – the equally incisive inner lives – depicted by Michael Nava, Walter Mosely, and Michael Connelly. He savored old masters like John le Carré, Patricia Highsmith, Alan Furst, and young torch bearers like S.A. Cosby and William Doyle. Not necessarily any of those latter names as direct influences (he wasn't much for spycraft or graphic violence), but he loved all those authors and he'd want me to mention their names.

While working within a gruesome tradition, my dad revered the high-spirited bonhomie of movies like *The Thin Man* and *My Man Godfrey*, preferring repartee from a nice mustache to much of the self-serious grime that followed the neo-noir of '70s. He also highly valued the filmography of the actor Divine. Again, not relevant, but not not relevant either.

Every one of the aforementioned names matter. Not just to illustrate the man's excellent taste (in 1974 he walked out of a Pittsfield matinee showing of *The Great Gatsby*, and demanded his money back because "that woman is not Daisy Buchanan!") but to illustrate the common thread connecting the disparate traditions my dad was working within; that of stories where stuff actually happens, where evil (even evil rendered in the smudgiest of grays) is generally frowned upon, and even occasionally punished, and all the suffering and violence that's baked into this world full of kicks is communicated – typically in less than 400 pages or a 120 minute run time – as the kind of fun that can only be found in barrels containing a surfeit of monkeys. My dad was a mystery writer and proud of it, who never once tried to defensively claim that his mysteries were different from other mysteries for some esoteric prejudice of small differences. My father subscribed to the belief that there was room in this world for Nick, Nora, and Asta to boot. While unbothered by snobbish distinctions, my father was no hack – partially out of a learned (and relearned) distrust of populism, and partly out of there being a limit to the amount of mass crowd pleasing one could reasonably expect from a series of gay gumshoe stories set in Albany in the 1980s. Especially when the series' dick swinging P.I. was only allowed one book (the one written in 1981) to slut out like a proper noir tomcat before everything went to hell. While not being a hack, instead writing with enough talent and bravery to document the AIDS era – from the orgiastic and innocent pre-HIV dream life of *Death Trick*, to the real-time wrestling with the epidemic's nightmarish reality in 1984's *On The Other Hand, Death* – with the epidemic as an intertwining presence and not merely as backdrop (without, conversely, allowing the staggering tragedy to overtake the plot), my dad would still always set out to entertain. Not as escapism, but in full awareness that his readership didn't need to be lectured about a decimation that they were living in the midst of, with no end in sight. They were reading a detective novel, with the accompanying expectation that, at least in fiction, there are some horrific mysteries that might be solved. Without shying away from the trauma necessary for a mystery novel to exist, or the hassles and cruelty endemic in society/life, Richard's way of taking on either was with a wry appreciation for the absurd and a moral compass

11

that buoyed rather than dragged. And when science finally found ways to battle AIDS, Richard continued to write stories – sometimes breezy and sometimes heartbreaking – with a culture's wake, rebirth, and growth into something akin to a hard-fought degree of comfort intertwined as unobtrusively into the entertainment at hand as the atrocity that came before was. My father's guiding principle was "we live in hope." At least that's how he signed off his emails. His second guiding principle was Elmore Leonard's dictum about taking out the boring parts. The guiding principles complimented each other. He was having a good time – as author, gay man, and someone who considered himself lucky to be alive as both. He wanted the reader to be having a good time too.

Under the pen name of Richard Stevenson, my father wrote nineteen books in total, with the last two of them published posthumously. The first novel published – after being scrawled out on those voluminous notepads and, as all the books written for the duration of their marriage were, typed up by my mom on some ancient noise box – was a thriller (co-written with Peter Stein) called *Grand Scam*. The gist of *Grand Scam* was, according to goodreads: "Oil-company security officer Ernie Hoopes is sure that women's land-speed record holder Liz Connerly, engineering genius Doug Swales, and suave former oil-company executive Larry Plochmann are responsible for hijacking twenty million dollars' worth of crude oil." If that plot summary doesn't make it clear, dad's first foray into mystery was a straight thriller in more ways than one. (Not that homosexuality precludes being a suave oil-company executive. But the book was published in 1978, when the inclusive and broadminded oil industry that we all enjoy today was still just a dream.) It was also the only one of Richard's books that his, otherwise quite sweet, mother would display on the family bookshelf, right next to Gore Vidal's *Lincoln*. After *Grand Scam*, my father began the Strachey series. Over the next two decades, as his children (me and my sister, Sydney) grew up and left home, Richard would document the sleuthings of Donald Strachey, an atypically (by the standards of Private Eye fiction, gay or straight, at the time) well-adjusted detective, as the hero navigated the gay underground and party-machine overground of Albany. Eventually, my dad had Strachey settle in Western Massachusetts; a region of bohemian placidity, where the Venn diagram overlap of "underground" and "overground" is a perfect bagel. There, as both detective and author grew older with a fair degree of aplomb, the reveries of the rolling Berkshire Hills would periodically be interrupted by murder, blackmail, or some other malfeasance summering in the area. Conveniently enough, the crimes Strachey was asked to solve often coincided thematically with some topical issue that both Strachey and his creator had strong opinions regarding.

The Strachey series was, first and foremost, a mystery series. With all the mayhem that requires. The Strachey books were also a sharing of space between a comedy of manners, the potential for which my dad saw as ingrained in nearly all social spheres, and the long-running and subtle character study that my father couldn't help but invest in as the relationship between Donald Strachey and his lover Timmy Callahan approached its fortieth year. But thirdly, as arguably a first among equals, the Strachey books are a travelog of current events. From the AIDS epidemic to marriage equality, from conversion therapy to the consolidation of media, to the almost quaintly anachronistic controversy over "outing" closeted gays, all the way to the (approximately) 1000 years that Donald Trump was in office (the possibility of which might having been a throwaway gag in any of the books written prior to the outlandish thing actually happening); if it was in the news, and if it was irritating to my dad, then there was probably a way to attach it – either as motivation or red herring – to some murder scheme that could only be solved by the most bemused of Private Dicks.

Richard's Berkshires are not The Berkshires of Summer homes or Edith Wharton old money. Well, sometimes they were; my dad ran in an economically diverse milieu, with both he and his husband occasionally open to a bit of dignified patronage, and he didn't kick gallery owners and art buying swells out of the metaphorical bed for eating metaphorical crackers. That said, the Berkshires depicted in the Strachey novels is a county not just of artisans, but of workers in general, most of whom make up the middle classes who staff the local high schools and precincts, or work as nurses – as my mother did – at the Berkshire Medical Center, and whose children wait the tables at the farm-to-kitchen restaurants, and work the counters at the high-end grocery stores that serve as the troughs from which vacationing New Yorkers feed (whilst Donald Strachey himself undoubtedly did the majority of his shopping at Price Chopper).

At the risk of virtue signaling my father as ostentatiously being part of a working class he never presumed to claim, with him not around to wave a single Elizabeth Warren bumper sticker in his own defense, I'll add that one of the (innumerable) tragedies that accompanied dad's cancer treatments was his losing his taste for McDonald's coffee, and it's at least some sort of kindness that the food at Friendly's went to hell long before dad's taste buds did. While certainly not averse to luxury, and certainly not one to overvalue hard work for its own sake, my dad operated from a core belief that some popular things are delicious, life should be more fair, assholes were running amok, but what else is new, and that neither the rich nor poor have any monopoly on tackiness. His detective consistently drank Sam Adams, which is nearly useless as a cultural signifier. Without giving too much away, most of the characters in *Chasing Rembrandt* end up getting just a bit shy of what they deserve (which, in its across-the-boardness, is a kind of justice). And the book has a surprising amount of baseball trivia for a guy who probably hadn't watched an entire game since the Phillies won the pennant in 1950. On the final pages, a character says "it's not a human life we're talking about here. It's just art." Which is a binary that, at any given time, depending on the day or hour, my dad may or may not have believed. To be honest, he was pretty keen on both.

I don't know where I was going with any of this. I'm terrifically sad that *Chasing Rembrandt* is the last Richard Stevenson novel, and I'm arguing with no one. Least of all my favorite debate sparring partner. You're here already, as a reader, and I really do appreciate that. You probably miss my dad. Not as much as I do, but it's not a competition. And I hardly need to convince you that, by dint of his adroit balancing of popular culture and high ideals, my dad was an artist, an empathetic observer of human foible and grace, an innovator in the field of letting gay characters, just, like, exist, just like any other crime fighter with a cool mustache. And my dad was a brisk, bracing, and hilarious storyteller, who believed in both living in hope and living in a world that's as corrupt as it is spilling over with simple pleasures, like cheap coffee and crime novels, and complicated pleasures as well, like art and human life and right and wrong and cracking wise in the shadow of death and all the other ingenious shit that makes a mystery a mystery.

Zachary Lipez,
January, 2023

Zachary Lipez is the son of author Richard Stevenson.

PROLOGUE

March 18, 1990, not long after midnight

IN BOSTON'S BACK BAY, a group of tipsy young people on their way home from St. Patrick's Day partying notice two men in police uniforms seated in a parked car outside the Isabella Stewart Gardner Museum. The small hatchback has no police markings, and one of the revelers surmises that something undercover is going down. Not wanting to interfere – or get hassled for underage drinking – the young man and his companions move on.

At 1:20 a.m., the two men in the car emerge. In the cool March mist, they walk up to the museum's side entrance and press the buzzer. Despite instructions never to do such a thing, one of the two guards on duty allows the not-really-cops to enter the building, in order, the guards are told, to "check out a disturbance." Soon, the guards have been tricked into being handcuffed, then wrapped in duct tape, and led to the museum's basement.

Over the next 80 minutes, the robbers wreak havoc, smashing the glass covers protecting masterpieces and slicing paintings out of their frames. They make off with 13 works, including three Rembrandts and a Vermeer, worth more than half a billion dollars and beloved in the world of art. It is arguably the greatest property theft in human history.

The hapless guards' descriptions of the thieves are vague. The perpetrators are said to be in their thirties, with one wearing what appears to be a fake mustache.

Although police and FBI investigators soon find many indications that mid- and low-level mobsters planned and carried out the audacious heist, no arrests are made and the art is not recovered, despite a $10 million reward offered for the safe return of the treasures.

The first real break in the case doesn't come until more than 30 years later, not in Boston but – unlikely as it first appears – in the small Western Massachusetts town of Lenox. And the woman who uncovers the disposition of the masterpieces is not a skilled and disinterested professional, but a non-official local woman with problems of her own.

CHAPTER 1

"THIS DOESN'T SOUND like a solution," I told Timothy Callahan. "It just sounds to me like adding to the problem."

"Yes and no," he said, giving me that little Indian head wobble he'd picked up on the Asian subcontinent back in his Peace Corps days. "The only serious downside is a short-term postponement of your having to go to work for Strathmore. And, Jeez, Donald, if this actually works out, financially speaking you'll be all but set for life."

"Oh, *if.*" I had another swig of my Sam Adams and noted that the foot resting on the deck railing had a sandal on it with a strap that had worn away nearly to the point of snapping in two. What did sandals cost now, anyway? It had been a while.

During our years together, Timmy had not been Mister On-the-one-hand-this-on-the-other-hand-that; I had. Far more often, he'd been Mister Yes-*or*-No, and he tended to disapprove of what he saw as my wallowing in the moral ambiguity of a bright and interesting but sometimes confused mind. But now we had a switcheroo?

"You could give it a week or so, and we could handle that financially," he said. "And if it didn't pan out, we'd still have had a nice visit to the Berkshires in the summer and you could go ahead and...do whatever you think you have to do. Sign on with Strathmore or whatever. And if it *did* work out

– I mean, God, Donald, it wouldn't just be lucrative for you. It would be a kind of gift to humanity!"

With the two of us sitting there on our Crow Street back deck on a balmy late June Albany evening, I mulled it over. In one way, Timmy sounded as though he was suffering from delusions of grandeur. Half of ten mil? Ha. But I also knew there was a lot of truth in what he said about his proposal resulting in something far larger than a mere cash bonanza.

For sure, I needed the money. I actually had a surprising amount of investigative work during the pandemic: going after embezzlers and pilferers – sometimes otherwise honest employees who were desperate for food and rent money. And naturally there was divorce work, often involving couples whose relationships had already been shaky, and being trapped in the same house or apartment for excruciating months on end had led to acrimony and worse. In some fraught situations, homicide had only just barely been avoided.

The problem was, too few of these clients had paid me in full, and I was all but broke. Two of the high-end restaurants that hired me to spy on thieving employees went bankrupt. Likewise a bowling alley. And a yoga center. Individuals who had employed me to report on their spouses' alleged virus-risky-fooling-around activities provided small retainers and then little or nothing more. They claimed penury. An elderly man I agreed to help was convinced that his young wife was sneaking out trying to contract Covid so she could bring it home and kill him with it and collect a sizeable inheritance. The old guy *did* succumb to the virus before he was able to pay me. Billing the widow didn't seem as if it would work.

A way out of my pandemic-related financial straits was to take a job recently offered to me by Strathmore Investigations, an outfit with offices around the planet that did mostly corporate work. But the company also helped out some characters in the Middle East and elsewhere on assignments that were rich in remuneration but otherwise nothing you'd want on your karmic resume. Timmy understood this conundrum all too well, and it was one reason he had been casting about for a money-making alternative for me that wouldn't embarrass both of us.

And then the business with the Gardner Museum art heist landed in his lap.

"Tell me again," I said, "why Kate Webster is so certain this thing is for real. On the face of it, it sounds preposterous. Yet I do understand that the Gardner paintings have to have ended up *somewhere*. So, I suppose, why not in Lenox? I guess it makes as much sense as any place."

"It's not just that Kate's Aunt Mary confessed on her deathbed to the whole thing about her son Bucky being one of the thieves. It's that when Kate went to retrieve the paintings in her aunt's house from behind Mrs. Costello's own big cows-in-a-field painting where Bucky hid them in 1990, somebody had gotten there first, ripped out the cardboard backing holding the masterpieces in place, and stolen them a second time. I mean, how much convincing do we need that this amazing thing is really for real?"

Timmy poured himself half a glass more of the Northern California beverage he had chosen to lubricate his part in our discussion. Among the many reasons he joined his boss, New York State Assemblyman Myron Lipschitz, in supporting anti-global-warming policies was Timmy's well-founded fear that his favorite Napa Valley vineyard would go up in flames.

"There is also the question," I said, "of payment, should I choose to get mixed up in this. It sounds as if I somehow succeeded in tracking down the great art works, I'd split the ten-mil reward with Kate. But if I failed, I'd get zip. Is that correct?"

He bent over to flick an insect off his bare knee and I had a good view of his expanding bald spot. Timmy was still as handsome as he'd been when we first met some decades earlier under a bush in Albany's Washington Park, but he now wore a baseball cap on the beach when visiting Provincetown to avoid severe top-of-the-head sunburn.

"The thing of it is," he said, "that financially speaking Kate has been hit as hard as anybody by the pandemic. After she lost her reporting job when *The Berkshire Eagle* had to cut back, she made a go of it for a while turning the house her mother left her into a B&B. But then Covid hit. And anyway, a whole lot of chain hotels have gone up in the Berkshires making it really tough on modest operations like Kate's. Sadly, Kate's husband Bill died in a bike-racing accident ten or twelve years ago. And her daughter Samantha can't help, because when the Peace Corps shut down the Thailand program on account of the pandemic, Sam and her boyfriend Travis took off for Fiji to regroup. And now they're more or less stuck there."

"A pity."

"Not that they'd be of much help. They wired Kate a couple of weeks ago asking if she could wire them four or five hundred."

"And did she?"

"Luckily, she had just had two unexpected bookings."

Strathmore was looking more and more inevitable.

"Anyway," I said, "it sounds like a kind of wild goose chase. It's all but certain the miscreant son Bucky was the one who snatched the great paintings from Aunt Mary's house. He'd stashed them there in the first place, and when his old mom passed on he thought he'd grab them before the cow painting they were hidden behind ended up at Goodwill or god-knows-where. A question, of course, is: why did he hide them there in the first place, and why didn't he retrieve them sooner?"

"Aunt Mary didn't explain any of that to Kate as the old lady lay in her room at Mount Mercy nursing home last Sunday night fading fast. Maybe because she didn't have the strength or presence of mind, or maybe she didn't really know. Bucky didn't even drive out to Lenox from Boston when she lay dying. The Sox were having a series of home games, and Kate said Bucky was so proud of never having missed a day of work in over twenty years."

"He's a groundskeeper at Fenway?"

"And a total Red Sox maniac. He has a huge collection of Sox memorabilia, especially Ted Williams. When Bucky was ten, his dad took him to a Sunday afternoon double-header. Williams was long-since retired by then, but he was sitting not far away from the Costellos in a box seat and Bucky snuck down and asked for the great man's autograph. Williams was famously cranky, and he told Bucky he was watching a ball game and Bucky should go suck a lemon. Bucky ran back to his dad crying. But he forgave Williams and kept on idolizing him. The Ted Williams fixation is just one of many examples, Kate told me, of Bucky's profound devotion to the Sox. It helps explain why even as his mother lay dying, he kept on keeping on – watering the grass and rolling up the tarps at Fenway. He's in his fifties now, and Kate says this is who Bucky somehow became, and he's just stayed that way."

"But three decades ago, he fit it into his busy Red Sox schedule to steal half a billion dollars' worth of art treasures?"

Timmy explained, "The team must have been on the road."

CHAPTER 2

"SO YOU NEGLECTED to mention that Kate's Aunt Mary was kind of barmy? Doesn't that fact hold a certain amount of pertinence?"

"Barmy might be putting it too strongly," Timmy said mildly. "Mrs. Costello was definitely a kind of New England eccentric. But Kate says she was more or less clear-headed most of the time. It's true, though, that one reason the Lenox cops didn't take Kate's report about her aunt's confession as seriously as she thought they should have was, they knew about Mrs. Costello's – let's call them *quirks*."

"Quirks, such as?"

We were on the interstate on the one-hour drive over to Massachusetts and the Berkshire hills. Timmy was driving his little Honda Fit and I was in the front passenger seat trying to straighten my legs.

"For instance, Mrs. Costello was not just an avid flower gardener, with her garden a well-known attraction around Lenox, with charities sometimes giving tours. She was also a Roman Catholic right-to-lifer who didn't just oppose abortion but also believed that flowers had souls, of a kind, and it was wrong to cut them and bring them into the house. Flowers in bloom should be left alone to live out their life spans and then wither on their own, she thought."

Timmy was one of those safe drivers who never took his

eyes off the road, so he did not turn to see the look on my face.

I said, "She must have considered florists agents of Satan."

"Another odd idea that she had," Timmy went on, "was more scientifically based. Mrs. Costello thought that too much of the leftover ice in drink cups that get tossed in the trash at fast food places was ending up buried in plastic bags in land-fills where it would remain for thousands of years. This water would not be reentering the hydrologic cycle to replenish the earth's supply, and this would lead to devastating droughts."

"Oh my."

"Kate said you had to give the old lady credit, though, for acting on her odd beliefs."

"How so?"

"She'd sometimes show up at the McDonald's over in the nearby town of Lee and root through the trash containers in search of discarded ice. Then she'd take it out and dump it in the parking lot so it could evaporate. The workers there knew her, and they'd been told to just look the other way when Aunt Mary practiced her environmental activism."

This was the woman who I was supposed to believe when she claimed she had three Rembrandts and a Vermeer hidden in her living room for over thirty years?

"I take it," I said, "that Mrs. Costello picked up a lot of her ideas on the internet."

"Oh, I doubt if she owned a computer. I know Kate said she didn't have a cell phone. She believed they caused brain cancer."

The June landscape along I-90 was gloriously verdant, and I thought even if this excursion degenerated into farce, I'd still have had this lovely late-spring outing. All the car windows were rolled down, and the aroma of new growth in woodlands and fields fed a feeling of hope despite what my ears were hearing and my brain was shouting.

At the town of State Line, Massachusetts, Timmy sig-naled, guided his small vehicle into the exit lane, and headed east toward West Stockbridge and Lenox.

"How come," I asked, "did anybody in Lenox take anything Mrs. Costello said all that seriously? Much of what you just described to me, Timothy, is well beyond eccentric, you have to admit."

Timmy continued to focus on the road ahead, adjusting his gaze only to take in the speed limit and other roadside signs meant to aid safe driving.

"Yes, Kate's aunt was definitely doty in the ways she was doty. But she was not only socially functional but quite popular, Kate told me, among her Lenox Garden Club pals and in church groups. People said she 'has her ways,' as they called it. But she was likeable – and quite honest."

"Quite honest except for one little thing?"

"It's true that when it came to Bucky, Kate's aunt's thinking could be undependable. She'd had to have a hysterectomy after Bucky was born, so he was her only child. All the Costellos thought she indulged him ridiculously. So did her relatives, the Winklemans, in Tyringham, where she's from. Everybody thought Bucky was a bad egg from an early age. But try telling that to Mary Costello. His dad tried to discipline young Bucky, Kate told me, but the kid would go bawling to his mom, and she'd say there, there, and always stick up for him. It was always a problem, and the family could tsk-tsk that Bucky was misbehaving, but that never stopped his mother from letting him get away with stuff."

"Stuff?"

"Kate will fill you in. When he was young, her cousin broke the law on a number of occasions."

"Prior to helping himself to an armful of the world's art treasures."

Timmy nodded. "It's not, though, that when it came to Bucky, Mrs. Costello was entirely without a conscience. That's obviously why before she died, she confessed about the hidden Gardner art to Kate. And to the priest."

"What priest?"

"On Sunday night, Aunt Mary told Kate about the art hidden in her house. Earlier that day a priest the nursing home had called came to hear the old lady's confession. Kate said her aunt told her she'd also confessed to the priest about her shameful complicity in the Gardner theft. She was clearing her conscience in the way she'd been taught as a Catholic through all of her eighty-seven years."

"So this priest knew that half a billion dollars' worth of great art was hidden behind *Sunday in the Park With Elsie* in Mrs. Costello's living room? I mean, Timothy – what the hell?"

A sign said *Lenox 6,* and Timmy turned left up a hill. "Hey, having an IQ above sixty, I am far from being somebody who thinks that priests can do no wrong. Of course, check this guy out. But surely it's Bucky himself who remains the chief suspect here. Am I not right about that?"

I said, true enough. But here was a fourth person who knew where the great art had been secreted. Were there still others?

CHAPTER 3

"DONALD, IT IS JUST SO kind and generous of you to help me track down the Gardner art on a – what do you call it? Contingency basis? I mean, I am so lucky! My psychotherapist is also seeing me without charging me. God, if only the Lenox tax collector was so understanding. My real estate tax payment is due the first of the month, and even if I could tell Town Hall I hope to be taking in ten million dollars in the near future and please hold off on dragging me into court, I'm sure they would just laugh. Which I'm afraid they should!"

We were seated on cushioned wicker chairs on the side porch of Kate Webster's big late-Victorian house on Undermountain Road having an iced tea. She was a tall, angular, middle-aged woman with a still pretty face now lined with worry. Her blond-and-gray hair was tied in the back with a silky amber scarf that looked Thai or Lao. Her most youthful feature – I guessed she was in her mid-fifties, like Timmy and me – was a pair of extra-large brown eyes that shone with thought and feeling. She was wearing an Indian-looking silver toe ring, and her leather sandals appeared even closer to collapse than mine. Kate's cat – she said his name was Arthur – was a black and white small mountain of a creature who crouched on a nearby milk crate thinking things over and paying attention to us only intermittently.

"I hope I can somehow help," I said. "It's quite the fantastic tale your aunt had to tell. Fantastic but I suppose not altogether implausible."

"As soon as I told Don your aunt's story," Timmy said, "he was intrigued and quite eager to be involved. I mean, maybe being part of history!"

Kate looked back and forth at us over the dark circles under her bright eyes. "It's kind of incredible, I know. But I knew Aunt Mary and I know Bucky, and it all just makes a kind of weird sense. That Bucky would do such a thing with Fess Tetlow, and then he'd panic, or whatever it was, and then hide the art they stole in his mother's living room. It's just so in character for him. And, yes, I know. God, do I ever know that Aunt Mary had a good many loony ideas. But they tended to be things having to do with her daily life, not something as far removed from Walker Street in Lenox as the Gardner art theft. I mean, really. I just can't imagine her making anything like that up."

I asked, "Who is Fess Tetlow?"

"Oh, did I not mention that ridiculous jerk?" She grimaced. "He was Bucky's partner in crime from the age of fourteen. This all goes way back. As boys, Fess and Bucky were a notorious pair around Lenox. For instance, they used to do things like suck the nitrous oxide out of the Reddi Wip cans in Lenox Price Chopper and toss the cans in the parking lot. And they shoplifted – tools and cologne and R-rated video tapes. When they were around sixteen, they took somebody's sailboat out on Stockbridge Bowl – they had no idea how to sail – and then they crashed it into a dock. Since the Tetlows didn't have a rupee to their name, Uncle Lewis had to pay the thousands of dollars in damages. The two managed to avoid being sent to jail, but they did have to pay fines on several occasions, and once they had to spend ten Saturdays washing the Lenox police cruisers. So, get the picture? When Aunt Mary said it was Fess who helped Bucky steal the Gardner art, it just sounded to me like déjà vu all over again – except really big time."

Timmy screwed up his face and sat nodding, guessing

what my next question would be.

"Was Fess Tetlow aware that after the robbery, the art was then hidden in your aunt's living room?"

"Oh God. Aunt Mary didn't say. And I didn't ask. At that moment, I was so flummoxed I was not at my interrogatory best. At the *Eagle*, my editor would have killed me."

"Where is Fess today? Any idea? And what's he been up to in recent years?"

"Oh, of course you're right. I've just been thinking Bucky, Bucky, Bucky. But absolutely Fess has to be considered a suspect. The guy really never quit being a criminal. I see his name in the paper once in a while in the District Court reporting. He lives down in Glendale, near Stockbridge. He might be in jail, though. I know there was a thing about some stolen TV sets from a delivery truck in North Adams. But, as for the Gardner art, I don't really know if Fess knew where the paintings were hidden."

"The guy should be easy to track down. If he's locked up somewhere, that will simplify things."

A light breeze picked up the aroma of a bank of lilac bushes in full bloom near our parked car, and I was glad again that I had made this visit – despite the fact that complications were beginning to accumulate.

Kate thought of something. "You know what? I doubt if it's Fess, in any case. He didn't have a key to Aunt Mary's house."

"There was no actual break-in?" Timmy asked.

"The Lenox police did go so far as to check the house for evidence of forced entry," Kate said, "and they didn't find any at all. The only real damage was Aunt Mary's smashed-up painting on the living room floor. That's just one more reason I think it must have been Bucky who stole – and then re-stole – the art. Bucky had a key to his mother's house."

"Did anybody else have one?" I asked.

Kate shook her head, and Arthur looked up briefly. "I think just Bucky and me and Aunt Mary. Oh, wait. I'm pretty sure Hank Thurmer would have a key. Yes, I'll bet he does.

31

Hank is Aunt Mary's handyman. He does gardening and helps out in the house, too, once in a while. Caulks windows or whatever. And Hank's a type who likes to come and go as he pleases, so I'm guessing he would have insisted on having his own key to the house. But Hank Thurmer *steal* anything? I would find that very hard to believe."

"It sounds as if your aunt had complete trust in Thurmer."

"She did, and with good reason. Hank is the straightest straight arrow you'll ever want to meet. In fact, some people think he goes too far sometimes with his ethical consistency. I know he complained to the Big Y Super Market headquarters that some customers at the market in Lee were not wearing masks when store rules required it, and whenever he went in the store, he'd confront people and make a fuss."

Hank seemed like a man worth having a chat with. "So, if your aunt trusted this guy so much, might she not have told him about the hidden art treasures? It sounds as if they were close, in a kind of way."

Kate chortled. "Close? No, I wouldn't use a word like that. I think the relationship was business-like, almost formal. Maybe it was a class thing, keeping their distance. There's a certain amount of that around here. Lenox had no trouble at all with pandemic social distancing since the concept was invented here in 1767."

"So Hank Thurmer was your aunt's handy man – but not candy man."

Neither Timmy nor Kate thought this was funny, and they gave me a look.

"Hank called me on Tuesday," Kate said, "after he heard the news about Aunt Mary's passing. He expressed his condolences and asked if he should keep on watering the garden. I said yes, sure, and then thought, oh God, will I be able to pay him? Anyway, he'll be at the house this afternoon at two if you want to talk to him. And I'm reasonably certain he'll be at the funeral on Saturday."

Now I wondered about something. "How come, Kate, the funeral is not until Saturday? That's five days from your aunt's passing. Aren't Catholic funerals generally held two or three days after a person's death?"

Timmy agreed. "Catholics are practically Jewish in that regard. Or Muslim. A two-day wake – three at the most – and then a final heave-ho."

Kate sighed heavily and Arthur blinked. "That's Bucky's doing. As next of kin on file at the nursing home, Bucky was notified before I was that Aunt Mary had died. He put Mount Mercy in touch with the McGonigal Funeral Home in Pittsfield. Then he called McGonigal's and asked them to hold off the funeral until Saturday on account of the Sox were at Fenway the rest of the week. Around here, of course, people would totally get that, and McGonigal's said no problem."

"So you have actually spoken with Bucky? I think Timmy mentioned to me that you had not."

Kate shifted in her chair and Arthur again opened his eyes for a brief second to take in this minor alteration in the human *mise-en-scene*.

"Oh, no. Speak with Bucky? Good grief, no. I tried and tried his cell and left at least ten messages. He's obviously refusing to speak to me, and I think we can all guess why. He lives with his current girlfriend Janice in Belmont, and apparently they don't have a land line."

Timmy piped up with what I was going to suggest next. "What about trying to reach him through the Red Sox office at Fenway? I mean it sounds like the Sox are practically his religion."

"He'll probably just refuse to take the call. But I suppose I should try," Kate had to agree.

"Nothing ventured," Timmy said.

Kate looked up the number on her phone, and we watched – now Arthur was paying attention, too – as she hit send.

"Hi," she told whoever answered. "I'm Kate Webster, the cousin of one of your employees, a groundskeeper by the name of Walter – normally called Bucky – Costello, and I'm trying to reach him concerning a fairly urgent family matter. Might Bucky be reachable there today?"

She listened, said, "oh. Oh my," and then rang off.

Looking borderline queasy, Kate said, "Crap."

"No luck?"

"Bucky isn't at Fenway. He called in sick early in the week. He hasn't been to work since Sunday. The woman I talked to said she hoped he was doing okay."

My guess was, he was.

CHAPTER 4

IT WAS DISAPPOINTING that Father Mike Thigpen wasn't going to be available, either. When I phoned the rectory where he lived in Pittsfield, the Berkshires' more populous county seat, I hoped I might chat with the priest and learn what he'd be willing to tell me – if anything at all – about Mary Costello's "confession." But I was told that Father Mike had gone off on a "retreat" in Vermont. He wouldn't be back for ten days.

Before meeting handyman Hank Thurmer at the scene of the most recent crime, as well as trying to locate the career thief Fess Tetlow, Kate led us to downtown Lenox for lunch at a sidewalk café on Church Street. The pleasant New England town was the same as I recalled it from earlier visits, with lots of pretty, well-kept, white frame houses with black shutters, some airy greens and small parks, and a commercial area with local non-chain businesses selling books, crafts, frocks, and fine or semi-fine art. Kate said a Mexican family had once moved in and painted their house red and yellow, but they soon relocated fifteen miles down Route 7 to Great Barrington.

Across the street from our café were a couple of art galleries, one featuring gorgeous Umbrian landscapes, and the other, the Sean Cunard Gallery, showing the work of a famous local metal sculptor. In addition to being on display at the Cunard Gallery, a few of Marcel Descantienne's stainless steel what-looked-like- bulimic-ballerinas had been placed curb-side up and down the street on brick peninsulas extending out from the sidewalks. Kate told us Lenox had redesigned its streetscape a few years earlier at great expense and instituted what she called "parallelogram parking."

Most of the pedestrians on Church Street had that distracted "what-shall-we-check-out-next?" look, a sign the Berkshires summer tourist season was well underway. Tanglewood, the Boston Symphony Orchestra's summer home, was not open yet but would start up soon. About half of the visitors we saw were wearing masks, the rest not. Many were staring at their phones as they ambled.

We all ordered fancy salads for a princely sum – Timmy offered to pay, and Kate and I said oh gosh, well, okay, *thanks* – and Kate and Timmy each had a glass of chardonnay.

I wanted to hear more about Bucky and his life in Boston in 1990, if Kate knew anything, but first we had to have the former-Peace-Corps-folks catching-up conversation. How is so-and-so? Have you heard from so-and-so? Is it true that so-and-so is in an insane asylum?

And then the stories, sometimes known as Timmy's 25 Stories. The time Sheldon from Brooklyn just couldn't cut it in the poultry development program because he failed as a chicken-sexer – learning to touch baby chicks' genitals and determine their sex so the males could be separated from the females and Indian vegetarians would never have to eat fertilized eggs. Or the time the Peace Corps official came from Washington and threw up on the District Poultry Officer's lap during a welcoming dinner. These ex-Peace Corps people were like a cult – Scientology-lite? – with their own rituals and tales and mythologies. I always felt left out, envious even, although after several decades, I almost felt I knew the stories well enough to pass.

I looked for a way to get back to Bucky, and after the two old pals wound down a bit, I jumped in. "Kate, your cousin Bucky was quite the busy young thief and vandal. But to your knowledge, he was never again arrested after the early juvenile offenses?"

"I don't think so. After he started working for the Sox in 1989, he seemed to have found the focus and purpose he needed to straighten out. At least that was Aunt Mary's story. The rest of the family never saw much of Bucky after that. But of course, the Gardner robbery was in 1990. So, really, who knows?"

I knew I could check Massachusetts arrest records for Walter Costello post-1989 and planned on doing so.

"Where was Fess Tetlow living in 1990? You said your aunt told you Tetlow was in on the theft."

"I guess he was in Boston then, too. I know in recent years Fess has been here in the Berkshires, because he has a way of getting his name in the paper with amazing frequency."

"Were Bucky and Fess ever violent, that you know of? It sounds as if the two were thorough-going fuck-ups, but at least not dangerous otherwise."

"I don't think Bucky would ever hurt anybody, but Fess I don't know. He was even more unstable and unpredictable than Bucky, but when he makes the District Court listings it's always for burglary. He doesn't seem to be violent, just hopelessly sociopathic and sneaky."

Timmy said, "I read that the two guards at the museum were tied up, but they weren't injured otherwise. In fact, there were suspicions for a while that one of them might have been in on the scheme. Some people still think so, though there's no evidence. And the guy certainly never had his financial situation improve in subsequent years."

Our salads arrived, handsome concoctions with grilled chicken on top of mine, salmon on Kate's and Timmy's.

Waving a chunk of salmon on a fork, Timmy said, "According to Wikipedia, in addition to the eight paintings that were taken from the Gardner, two other items were stolen. One was a French Napoleon-era eagle flag finial, and the other was an ancient Chinese vase. Did your aunt mention either of those?"

Kate shook her head. "No. But now I'm wondering if I

should take a look around the house. Though surely if Aunt Mary had possession of those valuable objects and knew where they came from, she would not have left them out in the open."

We all glanced up and down Church Street, as if we might spot a flagpole with an eagle on top or a suspicious-looking Chinese vase in a shop window. The only art object close by was one of the stainless-steel bulimic ballerinas, bent backwards as if meaning to hurl at the sky.

"We can all have a look," Timmy said. "I saw a picture of the vase. It's actually called a *gu* – a bronze vessel that was used on ritual occasions."

"If this valuable museum piece is in Aunt Mary's house," I said, "at least nobody needs to worry about her having stuck cut flowers in it."

Kate smiled wanly.

CHAPTER 5

"YOU TWO AREN'T FROM Lenox, are you?" The old man's tone bordered on hostile.

"No. Albany."

"You look kind of familiar. But I guess it's just a certain type."

"Well, we'll have to admit to that," Timmy said. I didn't know what he was talking about, and I don't think he knew, either.

Hank Thurmer certainly wasn't the "type" we expected. No work shirt, no grass-stained jeans, no vague aura of cannabis. Instead, he was an eighty-ish, short but ramrod-straight, clean-shaven, Nordic-looking fellow in pressed tan slacks, spinach-green dress shirt, and an awfully-heavy-for-the-weather tweed jacket.

"Over the mountain, we used to call it," Thurmer declaimed, glaring.

"What? Albany?"

"New York state. In my day, you could legally drink alcohol in New York at age eighteen. You look like you're too young to remember, and you probably never took the trouble to look into it. My younger brother Gordon and his high school cohorts went over the mountain to New Lebanon every chance they got, and nobody uttered so much as a peep about it. Totally inexcusable! Gordon died in 1997, his liver shot to hell, an alcoholic."

He peered at us accusingly, perhaps waiting for an apology from two emissaries representing Lucifer's Lair, the state of New York. We were standing on the front porch of Mary Costello's handsome white-with-black-shutters frame house on Walker Street, and Hank had just driven up in his Chevy pickup truck, which was waxed and shined to what I guessed its owner would have called a fare-thee-well. A clean blue tarp had been pulled tight over the truck's bed, perhaps concealing from view vulgar items such as rakes and hoes.

"I'm sorry to hear about your brother," Timmy said, and waited as Thurmer stared.

"I didn't know that about your brother," Kate added, gingerly stepping in. She had introduced us to Thurmer a few minutes earlier. "I know that liver disease can be a terrible thing to have to suffer through."

"Have to? There's a knee-slapper if I ever heard one. Nobody *has* to do anything, except eat frozen squash and die. Gordon did attend Alcoholics Anonymous in Pittsfield for a short period of time. And *that* was certainly a stupid idea. It's where he took up smoking. If his liver hadn't given out, I'm sure his lungs would've!"

Thurmer was glancing around now at the many flower beds, most of their plants not yet in bloom. Some white and lavender irises were still looking healthy, and the lilacs were at their peak. A nearby cluster of pink peonies had begun to open up, and I wasn't sure if the perfumed air we were all breathing came from them or from Thurmer's aftershave.

"Oh, would you look at that!" Thurmer blurted out. "Look at the ants on those peonies. Oh, Jesus wept!"

"What can you do about it?" Kate said, a note of hesitation in her voice.

"Not a thing!" Thurmer retorted. "It's the one thing your late aunt and I disagreed on. I would have sprayed the dickens out of those beautiful things with peppermint oil in water – perfectly safe for all concerned – but Mrs. Costello believed ants deserved a life too, and when you got her on that subject there was just no arguing. I told her, wouldn't those pretty flowers look even nicer if they aren't chewed up by those ugly black critters crawling around all over them? But, oh no. Even when the Garden Club came over, the ants were to be left alone. And nobody dared say a word. Everybody knew exactly which lines not to cross with Mary Costello, I can tell you that!"

Timmy said, "In India there's a Hindu sect called the Janes. As they walk along, they use a broom to sweep away any insects in their path so they don't step on them and kill them. Such is their reverence for life."

Thurmer paused to take that in. "Well, Mary Costello was no Hindu, that's for certain. I sat three rows behind her at St. Agnes's at eight o'clock Mass each and every Sunday. Your aunt had her funny ideas, Kate, but she was certainly not any-thing like what your friend here just said. In fact – oh, my – she'd've gotten a kick out of that one."

"Hank, let's go inside. You heard about the break-in. We were just wondering if you can make heads or tails of what anybody might have had in mind by wrecking Aunt Mary's big painting of the cows in South Williamstown."

"Yes, I heard from a friend of mine in the Lenox constab-ulary that you have this strange opinion some valuable paint-ings were hidden behind your aunt's pretty scene. A Norman Rockwell or something."

Kate didn't flinch, nor did she chortle. "Not Rockwell. Rembrandt. Vermeer. And some other great ones, too."

"Oh, really? I have to say that would be something for the town to crow about. But I don't believe it for a minute. I mean, sister, give me a break!"

Kate, Timmy, and I had already been inside the house briefly after our downtown lunch. Now we opened the screen door and Kate led Thurmer, Timmy, and me inside.

The house was eerily quiet – or maybe if we hadn't known of its owner's passing, just "quiet" – as we passed through the entryway and turned right into the living room.

"Great jumpin' Jehoshaphat!" Thurmer all but shrieked.

The wreckage of the cow painting was strewn across the floor in front of a fancy old Van Sciver sofa, the wallpapered wall above the piece of furniture bare. Even though the local police had not leapt into action when presented with this same sight two days earlier, Kate was determined to think of it as a crime scene and had not picked anything up.

"It sure looks like somebody didn't like that painting," Thurmer said, "though I can't for the life of me imagine why. I always thought it looked pretty. And what a mess you all left for me to clean up."

Kate explained that she didn't think it was a good idea to pick up the debris quite yet, which made Thurmer bristle again.

"Well, Kate, your aunt would just have a fit if she ever saw this. How long do you plan on leaving this mess here? A week? A month?"

"Not too long. And I can clean it up myself. I have a key to the house. By the way, you have a key, don't you?"

"Of course I have a key. And I brought it along with me in the event that you wanted me to turn it in."

"Not yet. We can be in touch about that. And about your continuing to maintain the gardens. If you want to do that. If it feels right without Aunt Mary to be here. Though I'm sure we can recruit some volunteers from the Garden Club for the time being, if it comes to that."

I could see into Kate's brain the budgeting that was going on and her fervent desire that Hank should maybe just choose to move along.

"Naturally I'll stay on. Why wouldn't I?"

"Well, actually Bucky will inherit the house. So it will be his decision about the garden upkeep. And about everything else."

Thurmer's steely blue eyes narrowed. "Bucky! That no-good? He'll be taking over? I find that very hard to swallow. I know your aunt had the habit of overlooking her son's character defects, but him owning this house and its nice gardens is just ridiculous! That would be criminal in itself."

"I haven't talked to Bucky about any of this, so we'll have to see. He doesn't seem to be around right now."

Thurmer stood up even straighter. "Of course that dipstick is around. What are you talking about? I just saw him yesterday."

"You did?"

I was driving past Fess Tetlow's filthy little house in Glendale, and I saw Bucky and Fess out in the driveway hollering at each other. I almost stopped and said, Hey, instead of aggravating the neighbors with this ungodly racket, why don't you spend your time cleaning up the old car parts and the other junk in this yard, Fess? But, thank the Lord, I knew better than to mess with the likes of those two, and I kept right on going."

CHAPTER 6

"OH FOR FUCK'S SAKE," Tetlow yelped, "Bucky's mom told somebody *that*? Oh, Jesus conniption fit! That all was – how many years ago? I mean, what the goddamn fuck? Christ on a cracker! I mean, I almost forgot about all that museum-paintings crazy who-the-hell-even-cares-anymore horse doo-doo. Anyway, it wasn't even Bucky's idea, that whole total waste of everybody's time. It was all Catchy's idea. Catchy hired us to do it. And then – holy shit! – Catchy up and croaked, and there we were with this garbage bag full of old art stuff and no idea what to do with it, on account of that was gonna be Catchy's job. And then the shitstorm! God, commotion like you'd never believe! Cops, FBI, fucking Walter Cronkite! You'd think we'd snatched Barbara Bush's crown jewels. And now Bucky's mom – Bucky's *mom*, of all people, turned rat? This is just un-fucking-believable!"

Timmy, Kate, and I had driven back to her house, where she phoned the court reporter at the *Eagle* and learned that although Fess Tetlow had a court date for a burglary charge in mid-July, he was not currently incarcerated.

Hank Thurmer had given me directions to Tetlow's home in the nearby village of Glendale, and I drove down in Timmy's car.

When Tetlow ambled around from the back of his house to ask me who I was and why I was there, and I told him, he just took another deep hit on the fat blunt his fingers had a good grip on and he proceeded to express his great astonishment.

"So then Bucky comes charging over here yesterday, and *he* thinks I know what happened to those pictures everybody was so freakin' freaking out about twenty years ago or whenever it was. He said his mom joined the majority on Tuesday, and I said I was sorry to hear that but she's with Jesus now. I said I didn't know what he did with the Gardner loot way back when, and I sure as fuck don't have a clue now, and anyhow I've got my own situation to deal with. Some Mexican stole some TVs, and the Berkshire County DA says I was in on it, but they can try and prove it, which they definitely will never ever do, not no way."

Tetlow's physical appearance didn't surprise me the way Thurmer's had - -in torn jeans and a beer-brand T-Shirt, Tetlow was a kind of middle-aged plumber's crack from head to toe - but Thurmer's description of Tetlow's house had been mostly accurate. A run-down single-story shanty-like structure in need of nine coats of paint and a new roof, it did have a sign out front, painted on a board nailed to a tree, that said *Our Cottage*. A sign on another tree said *No Trespassing Asshole*. Thurmer had been wrong about one thing. Instead of car parts strewn about, it was old ruined TV sets. There were 15 or 20 of them, big boxy appliances, pre-flat-screen.

Standing in Tetlow's driveway next to an oak tree that looked out of place with its stature and overall health, I was borderline enjoying the mild contact high from being this close to Tetlow's fumes. I was wearing a cheap white disposable mask, which might have kept any aerosol Covid from reaching my nostrils but seemed to welcome the pot micro-particles. Or was this wishful thinking?

I said, "Who was Catchy?"

Tetlow squinched up his pale pudgy face and thought this over. "Tell me again who you are?"

"Donald Strachey, a private investigator currently employed by Bucky Costello's cousin Kate Webster, trying to recover the Gardner paintings." I didn't say anything about the $10 million reward being offered by the museum. What would be the point?

"And Bucky's mom said the pictures were in her house? That's where Bucky stashed them after Catchy snuffed it? Bucky told me that yesterday, but I thought he was bullshitting me. Bucky can be such a bullshitter."

"The paintings," I explained, "were hidden in Mrs. Costello's house on Walker Street in Lenox. But it seems that when Bucky went there early Monday morning to get hold of them, somebody else who knew they were there had gotten there first and taken them away. He must have thought he had told you thirty years ago they were there. But you reminded him he hadn't told you?"

Tetlow shook his glassy-eyed head. "Bucky was *so* pissed off. I said, shit, Bucky, I can barely fucking remember anything I did last month, let alone back whenever all that shit went down. I said, Bucky, if your mom told your cousin you put the pictures in your mom's house, she must've told other people, too. Ask around, I said, but don't fucking come yelling at me, because I've got the DA and this Mexican crap of my own I gotta deal with. He left totally pissed off, but what can I do? I can do *fuck*, is what I can do."

"Who is Catchy?" I asked again.

"Yeah. Catchy. That's where Bucky needs to look." He stood there slowly thinking it over and then nodding.

"But you said Catchy died. No?"

Now some vigorous nodding. "He did. But he had this other guy, his assistant. We called him Catchy because he had this funny real name, Monmouth Khachaturian. He had this store on Newberry Street in Boston."

"An art gallery?"

"A lot of old pictures from France and what have you." Now he glowered. "Hey, look here, dude. If you repeat what I'm saying to anybody, I'll just say *prove it*."

"That's a strategy that seems to work for you, Fess." He seemed to have forgotten about his upcoming court date.

Tetlow had enjoyed another toke from his oversized blunt – it looked like a kind of weedy burrito that you smoked – and now he was confident and relaxed enough to go on.

"But here's the thing of how it all happened," Tetlow said conversationally. "Bucky and I went to some rich guy's house in Weston that Bucky had tickets to from the Sox. It was a party on Ted Williams's birthday, and maybe he was gonna be there, but he never showed. Anyway, some other players were at this blow, and Bucky wanted to go. On the way out the door, Bucky saw this thing on the wall, a little drawing in a gold-looking frame. He said let's just grab that, it might be worth something. Nobody was looking, so we did. Bucky just stuck it under his coat."

More fumes wafted my way, which I enjoyed.

"Then," Tetlow said, "what are we gonna do with this picture thing, done by some French guy? So we go into this store on Newberry Street with stuff like the picture we had with us in the window, and maybe they'll take it off our hands for a couple of hundred or whatever. I mean, what'd we know?"

I understood. "What was to lose?"

"So, Catchy – he's this white-headed grandad with a big gut all duded out in his Sunday best – Catchy says, Hey, where'd you lads get ahold of this? Bucky says, Well, that is for us to know and you to find out. Catchy says, You tell me the truth and I'll give you two hundred bucks for this item. And I have another idea with an even bigger payoff for you boys if you're interested. Then Bucky says, yeah, we snatched this thing in Weston, and what are you going to do about it? And what else do you have in mind, Catchy? Bucky started calling him Catchy that first five minutes."

As I stood there listening, I thought, yes, this makes sense. Art history in Boston changed for the worse not at the hands of an evil genius but at the hands of a crooked art dealer and two overgrown juvenile delinquents. Even Rembrandt can be touched by the banality of evil.

"So, to make a short story shorter, Catchy asks some more questions like if we ever stole anything from a museum.

Bucky says oh yeah, lots of times, pictures of cows and naked women, which of course was total BS. But this guy saw what we had snatched in Weston and he believed Bucky. Then Catchy tells us about this museum with a lot of expensive stuff in it, and it has lousy security and it would be easy to rip the place off. He says if we do it, he'll give us five thousand each as soon as he fences the pictures – he's got some people out of town he knows who will take it off his hands. The thing is, Catchy says, if we get caught, we're on our own. He'll say he never saw us before in his entire life."

"Nice guy."

"Hey, we got that. Like, if you go running to the Berkshire County DA and tell her anything I just said, I'll say I never laid eyes on you, not even once. So don't get any ideas. But if you can get any of those paintings back and put them back in that dump of a museum, hey. It's no skin off my nose."

"What you've told me should help."

"Is there a reward?" Tetlow asked.

"It's my impression there is."

"Shit. Maybe that's why Bucky is so het up. But they sure as fuck aren't going to give it to *him*."

"I wouldn't think so."

"Anyway, I told him, yeah, Catchy is dead, but what about that other guy? He knew about the heist, because I know Bucky called him after Catchy croaked. Bucky said what should we do with the pictures – they're in a garbage bag in Bucky's backseat – and how do we get paid? The asshole pretended he didn't know anything about anything, but Bucky said he knew, all right. And if he didn't, he sure as hell knew after Bucky phoned him at the art gallery."

"This was Monmouth Khachaturian's assistant?"

"Miles Tate was his name. When I mentioned him to Bucky yesterday, Bucky said, yeah, that guy. I've been thinking a whole lot about him. I'm thinking, Bucky says, that this is the motherfucker I have to find."

CHAPTER 7

"SO IT LOOKS AS IF Bucky mostly just wanted to check Fess out and eliminate him as a suspect in stealing the Gardner art from your Aunt Mary's house, and Bucky thinks this Miles Tate character is the most likely present-day bad actor. After meeting Tetlow, I'd have to agree that Fess is not at all who we're looking for here. The guy had no key to the house, and he's such a stoner doofus that for him picking a lock would be like neurosurgery for the rest of us."

Kate, Timmy, and even Arthur were rapt with attention.

"At least now we know how the original heist was carried out, and that alone is just such an extraordinary thing. I mean, after all these years, who'd've thought?"

They both looked at me, not moving, all but goggle-eyed.

"Even though Tetlow will deny up and down everything he told me if the cops or the FBI ever interview him, it's all highly credible information that Tetlow has, and Bucky has, and we now have, and Bucky doesn't know we have it."

Timmy was twitchy with excitement – a rarity for him in recent years except when he was re-watching Satyajit Ray's *The Apu Trilogy* – and he was alternately nodding and shaking his head and trying to process it all.

Kate, though, looked as if she wasn't sure how much to be excited and how much perplexed. "But who on earth is Miles Tate? I mean, if Bucky is right that he's really somebody who would know the art was hidden in Aunt Mary's house thirty years after the fact of the robbery. I don't get that. And I don't think there's any Miles Tate around here, though we can check."

"And anyway," Timmy said, "how would this guy have gotten into the house without a key? Unless he was some kind of cat burglar. Though according to Tetlow, Tate was an art gallery assistant, not a lock-picking acrobat."

We were back on the side porch, the scent of the lilacs in late afternoon pleasantly heavy in the air.

"What if," Kate said, perking up again, "Miles Tate became somebody else? He changed his name and whole identity, and he's right here in Berkshire County living among us?"

Timmy made spooky-music noises. "That's creepy. Though on second thought, it's not all that far-fetched. He's around here and he's somebody your aunt might have confided in. Like, for instance, the priest she told about the hidden paintings."

Kate liked this idea. "Maybe Father – what's his name?"

"Mike Thigpen."

"But he wouldn't have a key," Kate said.

"If it's like the one in Albany," Timmy said, "the Archdiocese is practically penniless. The ten-mil reward would be quite a financial shot in the arm for them. It could be some kind of Augustinian notion of a bad act for a larger good."

"I seriously doubt Aunt Mary would have given him a key to the house along with her confession. Anyway, she wanted *me* to retrieve the paintings and return them to the Gardner. I really think she might have been counting on me to do this huge good deed and get her out of Limbo."

Arthur suddenly leaped from his perch on the milk crate, stretched, and hopped down the steps to the parking area, where he stood staring straight ahead.

"Anyway," Timmy said, "it was Mount Mercy who called Father Thigpen in. He didn't just show up. Plus, I never heard of a priest who was a locksmith. Or a cat burglar, either. When priests go off the rails, their sins are either more exotic or more mundane, or a combination of the two."

Kate said, "Seriously, though. Not the priest, but maybe somebody else who could pick a lock? Of course, how would anybody else even know that the Gardner art was hidden in the house? And behind the cow painting in the living room?"

"Right," Timmy said. "Somebody who either knew Miles Tate or *was* Miles Tate."

We were sipping iced tea with mint leaves that we had picked earlier in Kate's yard. I assumed this would have been okay with Mary Costello, eating garden items that did not, as far as I knew, blossom in any major way.

Timmy asked, "Might your aunt have told somebody at the nursing home about the hidden art? Was she close to anybody there? Staff or other residents?"

Kate sighed. "I would doubt that very much. She'd been there for about six months, following her stroke in January. She had a couple of roommates, but she didn't like either one. One of them she complained about after the old lady's daughter brought in a big bouquet of gladiolas. Aunt Mary had to be moved to another room. She said the staff were nice people, but I didn't get the impression she was close to any of them. Sometimes she was confused, though, and I suppose it's possible she blurted something out to somebody and then didn't remember doing it."

"Unless it turns out," Timmy said, "that the head nurse at Mount Mercy is married to a locksmith, that situation looks unpromising."

Kate looked grim. "It does seem like we're at a dead end. I'm baffled."

"The one person who really knows what's going on here," I said, "is Cousin Bucky. What's next is, I need to find him, and we have to have a talk."

"The only phone number I have," Kate said, "is his cell and he won't answer my calls. Maybe you could try your luck, Donald."

"Face to face would be better. It would be harder for him to refuse to say anything at all. What about the girlfriend?

Her name is Janice?"

"I know she's a waitress at a Friendly's in Belmont. Aunt Mary said something about that one time. Aunt Mary said Bucky had told her about Janice and how Janice was a religious woman and a good Catholic."

"Do you know her last name?"

"No idea," Kate said. Arthur hopped back up the steps and sat looking up at Kate expectantly.

"How many Janices could there be working at Friendly's in Belmont?"

Timmy said, "Probably no more than twelve."

I got out my phone to look up the number for a Friendly's restaurant in the Boston suburb of Belmont. I noticed I had a text from Laurel Peaseley, my contact in HR at Strathmore Investigations. She said she was wondering if I'd had enough time to consider the company's offer of employment. In any case, she said, there were others interested in the job, and would I please respond with my yes or no by Friday? That was 48 hours away.

Arthur continued staring up at Kate, who was paying attention to me – I appreciated this; the cat was going to have to wait – as I phoned the Friendly's on Primrose Road in Belmont. I said, "May I please speak with Janice? I'm afraid it's a family emergency."

"Janice Nestor or Janice Nurdlinger? They're both on shift."

I held the phone away from my mouth and said, "*Mumble mumble.* Her current life partner is Bucky Costello, if you know who I mean."

"Yeah, Janice Nestor. This is not a good time, but if it's an emergency, hang on."

After a minute of restaurant kitchen noises, a female voice came on the line.

"Who's this? Emergency? What emergency? It's not Dad, is it?"

"No," I said, "not to worry. Sorry to bother you at work, and I'll be quick."

"You freakin' better be. I've got nine booths and a counter."

"My name is Donald Strachey and I'm employed by Bucky's cousin Kate Webster. I badly need to contact your partner Bucky Costello about his mother Mary. You probably know she passed away on Tuesday."

"Bucky! That asshole!"

People kept calling him that. "Why do you say that, Janice?"

"I'm sorry about his ma, but that lowlife helped himself to four hundred dollars from my Disney World fund that I keep with my unmentionables, and then he friggin' took off and I haven't seen him since Tuesday. I called Fenway, and they said he was sick. Sick! Bucky is sick, all right. He's a thief and he's a jerk, but sick he ain't except when he feels like it. I've about had it up to here with Mr. Costello. I've said that before, and this time might just be one time too many!"

"What do you mean by he's a thief?"

"Hey, I gotta go. I'm mean, criminy! He took my four hundred – I told you that. He called yesterday, and he gave me some line of bull about somebody stole something from *him,* and he had to get it back. Something worth a lot of money, but I've heard those stories before. I said, oh yeah, is it worth more than four hundred dollars? And Bucky said plenty more--and anyway he isn't even sure who has this valuable thing, some mystery man or something."

"Mystery man?"

"Somebody Bucky knew a long time ago and maybe changed his name or something. Some man, Bucky has his phone number but not his name – which I do not understand at all. Look, I'm getting the evil eye from my supervisor, so I gotta hang up. Good luck finding Bucky and give him a piece of my mind for me. And I want my four hundred back ASAP!"

"Did he say where he is or where he was planning to go?"

"He said he couldn't tell me. Which is unusual. He always tells me where he's going, and it's always the same place. To work. At the bleepin' ball park. So I guess he does have some new trick up his sleeve. Some trick he thinks is worth over four hundred dollars. You know, he didn't even apologize for filching the twenty twenties? He said it was an investment. God, Bucky is such a bullshitter!"

"Did he mention if he would be at his mother's funeral in Lenox on Saturday?"

"Oh. I suppose he will. Maybe you can talk to him there."

Naively, I said that sounded like a plan.

CHAPTER 8

"OH CRAP, NOW I'M GETTING a migraine."

Kate was just off the phone with the funeral home in Pittsfield.

"They said Bucky called them and said he probably would not be able to attend his mother's funeral on Saturday because of commitments with the Sox. We *know* that is total B-S."

Timmy said, "Uh oh."

"And that's not all. Maybe you heard me in the kitchen. I had to give McGonigal's my credit card number. Bucky told them he was not able at the present moment to put a deposit toward the funeral because he was waiting for a large amount of money he was expecting to come in. He said his cousin would do the deposit and he would work it out with her later. His cousin – that would be *me!*"

I said, "We have to find the guy. It sounds as if he does have a good idea who has the Gardner art. According to Janice, he just doesn't know where this person is or maybe even what the person's current name is. It does sound as if it's Miles Tate Bucky is after."

Timmy agreed. "It has to be this Tate guy. Or somebody else connected with Khachaturian but who didn't take part in the actual operation. There were just the two robbers, but the police and the FBI think it was put in motion by mobsters,

I read. The mob is behind a lot of art heists. They then offer to quietly sell the art back to the museums or collectors they stole the stuff from for a fraction of its value. And the owners are often willing to do it. Mobsters also use stolen art to bargain with prosecutors to get shorter sentences or even no sentences at all for fellow criminals. This has been known to happen in Boston. And it sounds as if Khachaturian had connections to those kinds of hoods."

"Don't rich private collectors sometimes hire thieves to steal stuff for them?" Kate asked. "So they can hang great art in their hideaways and just look at it themselves? Or show it off to their immoral wealthy friends?"

"Sometimes it works that way," Timmy said. "But historically museum thefts are more lucre-driven than esthetics-driven. After the Gardner heist, the FBI thought there was a Philadelphia mob connection, but they investigated and nothing ever came of it. The Boston cops thought it was all local wise guys. But they were sort of shoved aside by the feds – a mistake, according to a *Boston Globe* reporter who covered the crime. It was the local cops who really knew the Boston mid- and low-level mob scene."

Kate was massaging her own head, and if she had a migraine, I hoped she had something to take for it. We were all guzzling iced tea and were plenty caffeined up, probably not helpful, I thought, for a bad headache.

Kate said, "Bucky was used to casually breaking the law. Certainly when he was young, stealing just seemed kind of second nature to him. But Aunt Mary was convinced that once he started working for the Sox, he changed for the better. I know she even helped him out financially when he got serious about collecting Red Sox memorabilia. When he was kid, he kept his baseball cards under his bed in shoe boxes, and whenever I came over, he'd get them out and tell me who each player was. And he had memorized all their statistics. RBIs and home runs and all that kind of thing."

"I never collected sports stuff," Timmy said. "I did have a scrapbook with pictures I cut out of magazines with Johnny

Sheffield as Bomba the Jungle Boy. I guess that was a clue as to something about me. But at the time, what did I know?"

"Too bad Bomba didn't go to Georgetown when you were there," I said, "and you were older and had become more self-aware and more available."

"No, but Freddie Pringle was there. And he liked to parade around in the dorm hallways in a Bomba-style loincloth."

"And even popped into your room from time to time, you once told me. To whisper in your ear about life in the jungle."

"I had managed to figure some important stuff out by then."

Kate looked as if her migraine was getting worse, but she might just have been bored by the turn the conversation had taken.

She said, "It's hard to imagine Bucky actually becoming part of organized crime. He and Fess were just a couple of screwed-up delinquents. And even in Boston, with its many opportunities for mob connections, I just don't think he had the right personality for that. And what if Aunt Mary had somehow found out? Bucky would not have taken a chance on her thinking he'd become an actual Mafioso. He would not have risked breaking her heart like that. No, I think something else happened that led to him robbing the Gardner."

"It sounds," I said, "as if your cousin was as fervent a Red Sox fan as your aunt was a fervent Catholic."

"It's true that the Sox sort of became Bucky's religion. I know he has some ideas that are bordering on the spiritual. Or just plain goofy, many would say. I know Bucky was so happy when Ted Williams died and his grown children disobeyed his wishes to have his ashes scattered in the Florida Keys where Williams liked to fish. Instead, they had him cryonically frozen, his head separated from his body, so that on the day medical science could cure him of the disease that killed him, the great hero of New England sports could be brought back to life. Bucky wanted Williams to see the Sox win another pennant, or even the World Series, and Bucky was totally convinced that on some future great day this miracle would actually come to pass."

"If it's not Miles Tate," Timmy wondered, "could the mystery man with the Gardner art treasures Bucky is trying to track down be some kind of sports figure?"

"Sports. Art. Religion. Take your pick." Now I was starting to get a headache, too.

Timmy said he'd read there was an especially good book about the Gardner heist, and maybe we could pick up some clues in there. See if "Catchy" is mentioned. Or even Miles Tate. He said it was written by the *Globe* reporter who knew the heist story inside and out.

Kate said, "Let me check. The Bookstore might have it. It's a great bookstore, in town, run by a guy who once worked at the Gotham Book Mart and knew Marianne Moore and Man Ray and young Patti Smith, and who can recite all of Groucho's best lines."

Kate picked up her phone, and Timmy said, "My favorite Groucho line is, 'The secret of life is honesty and fair dealing. If you can fake that, you've got it made.'"

"I just hope," Kate said, as she waited for her call to The Bookstore to be answered, "that later we won't be repeating another good Groucho line: 'I had a wonderful evening. But this wasn't it.'"

CHAPTER 9

THEN OUR LUCK TURNED again. Not only did The Bookstore, on Housatonic Street, around the corner from where we'd had lunch, have in stock the book about the Gardner theft that we wanted. But we ran into a friend of Mary Costello on the sidewalk out in front of the store.

"Kate, oh goodness, I am so sorry about your aunt. We all knew she was in a precarious state, but it's still hard to believe that that remarkable personality is no longer with us."

Kate introduced Timmy and me to Myrna Barkley, a Lenox Garden Club cohort of her aunt's. She didn't mention why we were in town, just saying Timmy was an old Peace Corps friend.

"Oh, the Peace Corps. JFK. Is that still going?"

"Yes, but it's shut down during the pandemic."

We were all wearing masks. Kate's, Timmy's and mine were plain white. Myrna Barkley, a slight, neatly dressed woman in her seventies, had on a handmade mask with an image of scarlet azaleas on it, making it look as if her lower face was hemorrhaging.

"I kept meaning," Myrna said, "to visit Mary in the nursing home. But with one thing and another – my granddaughter's college graduation, Martin falling down the porch steps in April, and then all this Covid craziness – I just never made it over there. You know how it is."

"Of course."

"I don't know about Martin. He's still limping. And doing plenty of complaining, naturally. But I'll be at the funeral on Saturday. So many of the Garden Club gang is passing on. It's all so sad, really. The membership is down and we don't seem to be getting enough new recruits. And to lose a stalwart like Mary Costello is a particularly unfortunate loss."

"She was quite the flower gardening devotee, that's for sure," Kate said.

"So, what will become of the house and gardens? Will you inherit that? Or Mary's son? What was his name?"

"It's Bucky, yes. He is Aunt Mary's heir."

"Oh. Well. Bucky. Yes. Anyway, I need to return my key. Can I just give it to you? You can pass it on. Would you mind?"

Kate stared. "Key?"

"To Mary's front door. You wouldn't know, necessarily. Several of the Garden Club gang have keys to your aunt's house so we can drop off plantings or seed catalogs or what-not when nobody's home. Drop off, or, in Mary's case, more often pick up. I don't have the key with me, but I can give it to you on Saturday at the funeral, if that's all right."

"You haven't gone into the house since Aunt Mary died, have you?"

"No. Why would I?"

Kate looked as if she was having a hard time keeping from grabbing Mrs. Barkley and shaking her. "Well, there was actually some vandalism at the house. I'm sure you had nothing to do with it, Myrna, but I just wondered if you had seen anything going on there that struck you as odd."

"Oh, no! Not Mary's new planters, I hope, for her yellow roses!"

Timmy and I were listening with great interest to this exchange as customers meandered in and out of the bookshop next to us. Nearby on the sidewalk was one of Marcel Descantienne's steel wraiths looking ecstatic.

"No," Kate said, "it was my aunt's painting that she did herself that hung in the living room. The one with the cows in a field. Someone got into the house and wrecked the painting."

"Oh, for goodness sakes! Why would anybody do that? That's horrible!"

"We have reason to believe that some valuable objects were hidden behind the painting, and that's what the person was after."

"What? Stocks, or bonds, or something?"

Kate didn't want half the people in Lenox to know the truth about the Rembrandts and Vermeer and start chasing after the $10 million reward that she – and I – wanted so badly to get our mitts on. And Mrs. Barkley apparently had not heard what Hank Thurmer had picked up from his cop friend.

"No bonds," Kate said. "Just some other art that's considered valuable."

"That's such a shame about the cow painting," Mrs. Barkley said. "Your aunt was a competent amateur painter."

"Maybe," I put in, "one of the other Garden Club members who has a key to the house noticed something that could help us out. Can you tell Kate who those other people might be?"

Somewhere behind the azaleas, she screwed up her face. "I suppose I could. But it does seem if any of the gardeners had seen anything amiss, they would have phoned the rest of us – or even reported the incident to the police. And none of our gang would have been the culprits, surely. We're all honest people. Kate, I'm sure you know that."

"I do."

"We did have a member for a while, Marilyn Hurst, who had some serious anger issues. But she moved to Greenfield last year. Anyway, she wouldn't have had a key. Nobody trusted her, really. Marilyn's husband had some financial conflicts with his law firm – hand-in-the-till type of shenanigans, I was told – and I always believed Marilyn was just as shifty as Edward was."

Mrs. Barkley named the five Garden Club members that she knew would have a key to Mary Costello's front door. Kate said she knew all of them, if only to say hello to, and she would give each of them a call.

"Yes, or I'm sure you'll see them at the funeral," Mrs. Barkley added. "Oh," she exclaimed through her scarlet mask. Her diction was good and we didn't have to struggle to comprehend her when she enunciated through her colorful floral display, "There is another thing maybe you don't know about, Kate, and it sounds as if you probably should."

"Oh? What's that?"

"The key under the rock."

"What is the key under the rock?" Kate's face suddenly tightened, as if her migraine might be worsening.

"Under the hydrangea bush next to the front steps, there's a small rock. Under the rock, there's a key to the front door. Mary put it there when she locked herself out of the house one time with her car keys and all her other keys locked in the car. This is when she was still driving, of course. Mary knew she was getting forgetful, poor thing, and she didn't want to take any chances. Of course, with her bad back she had a hard time bending down to get at the key under the rock. She told me one time when she locked herself out, she got down on the ground and couldn't get up, and she had to crawl up the front steps on her hands and knees. I wanted to laugh when she told me. But I kept a straight face, since I don't think she thought it was funny at all."

"Who else would know about the key under the rock?" Kate asked.

"I have no idea. Probably very few people, would be my guess."

Kate said, "Very few. I'm certainly glad to hear *that*."

CHAPTER 10

"BUT JANICE THE GIRLFRIEND said Bucky was searching for some 'mystery *man*,'" Timmy pointed out, "not 'mystery elderly woman.' So the Garden Club gals sure don't look like any of them is the person Bucky is after. Or are people we need to concern ourselves with at all, probably."

"It's possible," Kate said, "that Bucky said 'mystery woman' but Janice heard 'mystery man.' Anybody's mind can work that way."

We were sitting around Kate's kitchen table finishing up the fig and prosciutto pizza we'd picked up in town earlier. Arthur was dozing on the kitchen counter next to the microwave, which Kate said he liked to snuggle up to. She told us a B&B guest had once complained to the Board of Health that her cat habitually lounged about in a food preparation area. But when an inspector came around, Arthur had gone out for a walk, so nothing ever came of that.

Kate had already phoned three of the Garden Club key holders – Sally Ferber, Mitzi Mankiewitz, and Georgine Moss – and none had said anything remotely suggesting they had somehow been up to no good. All expressed condolences over Mary Costello's passing, and all seemed genuinely shocked, Kate said, that her aunt's house had been entered and the cow painting destroyed. None had yet heard the rumors about missing valuable art. I would have liked to interview each of these ladies myself, but that didn't seem urgent, and it was postponed for the time being.

Two other key holders – Carla Mariori and Peg Williamson – could not be reached, and Kate left messages asking them to phone her.

"Anyway," Kate said, looking a bit less physically put upon – she had slugged down a pill for her migraine – "God knows how many other people knew about the key under the rock. Two people? Twenty-five? Five hundred? Good grief, where does that leave us, really?"

Timmy had been speed-reading the book we'd picked up in town, *Master Thieves: The Boston Gangsters Who Pulled Off the World's Greatest Art Heist*, by Stephen Kurkjian, the *Globe* reporter who'd become the New England expert on the great crime.

It was the author's idea, Timmy told Kate and me, that gangland figures had for years seen the low-security Gardner Museum as ripe pickings for a lucrative art heist. One theory was that the two men who pulled off the job under orders from a mob higher-up died a year after the theft in a gangland shooting. There were a number of theories as to who any higher-ups were. A prime candidate was a sometime crook named Robert Gentile. The FBI believed he'd hidden the masterpieces under a false floor in a shed on his Manchester, Connecticut property. But nothing was ever found there – or anywhere else.

Nowhere in the Kurkjian book, Timmy said, was there any mention of a Fenway Park groundskeeper and a screwed-up burglar from Glendale. Nor of a Newberry Street art dealer named Monmouth Khachaturian or his assistant Miles Tate.

"Janice told me," I said, "that Bucky was looking for somebody he knew a long time ago who had maybe changed his name. It would be a waste of time, though, for us to start looking for Boston mob figures – either high-level or low – who might have changed their identities thirty years ago. We could spend months chasing leads. We could even be talking about people in the Witness Protection Program, and I have no way of accessing that information. So Miles Tate is still our best bet. For what that's worth."

"So, are we stuck?" Kate wondered.

"Maybe, but maybe not. Kate, give me Bucky's cell number, please."

She looked at me curiously, but Timmy saw what I was doing when I got my own phone out.

"Good idea," Timmy said.

"It's an app called Spy-oh-my," I explained to Kate. "As long as Bucky's phone is on, the app will tell me where he is within a few hundred yards. If he stays in one place long enough and I'm lucky enough, I can speed to wherever he is and then either confront him and find out what I can. Or I can follow him until he finds the mystery man who may have the art treasures in his possession."

"Wow. Modern technology. I thought only the government could do stuff like that. It's good, but it is also pretty creepy."

"The trick will be catching Bucky with his phoned turned on. I'm hoping he is uninformed about this type of device and won't keep his phone off except when he's using it. It will also be important that he isn't hours away, or constantly on the move."

"Well, great! Let's try it," Kate said with enthusiasm, making Arthur briefly check us all out.

Kate recited Bucky's number, and I keyed it into my phone and activated the app.

The phone rang, and a gruff voice came on saying, "Leave a message." Bucky did not answer in person, but his device was in fact turned on. It showed that he was back in the Boston area, in the town of Concord. So, what was he doing there?

CHAPTER 11

WHAT WITH CONCORD BEING a two-hour drive across the state from Lenox, I did not commandeer Timmy's car and rush out there. Bucky might have moved on by the time I arrived, or he might have turned his phone off. Anyway, my Spy-oh-my would only locate the general vicinity of Bucky's phone. If I had been able to get hold of his smart phone and hide a Spy-oh-my tracking device in it, I would have known exactly where he was. But what I was working with was far less precise.

Still gathered around Kate's kitchen table, we set out conducting a search for any trace of Miles Tate. First, Kate phoned a friend, Melissa Craigie, who ran an art gallery in nearby Great Barrington. Kate knew that Craigie had worked in a Boston gallery two or three decades earlier. Without saying why she wished to know – she just said it was an inquiry on behalf of a friend – Kate asked if Craigie knew of a Miles Tate, who worked at the Khachaturian Gallery on Newberry Street in 1990. Craigie told Kate, no, the name didn't sound familiar, although she dimly recalled a gallery run by a man named Khachaturian. She did have, however, a friend in Boston she could call who knew the Newberry Street art scene better than she did. Craigie said she'd call Kate back when she had learned anything.

Second, Kate called a friend she'd worked with at *The*

Berkshire Eagle in Pittsfield. She asked her pal, an editor named Greg Herkimer, if he'd do a LexisNexis search for a Miles Tate. He said sure. He said he was kind of busy trying to get the next day's paper put together, but he'd call her back when he could.

While we waited, hoping to hear from anybody at all, I swigged from time to time from a bottle of Azerbaijani beer one of Kate's guests had left behind, and I did my own online search for Miles Tate. I came up with nothing at all. Timmy eschewed any beverage beyond Lenox tap water. He had had a glass of wine with lunch and meant to soon be driving us both back to Albany, so he erred on the side of caution – as he did in most areas of life, bless his ethical conventional heart. Kate had a ginger ale.

"Maybe," Timmy said, "you should talk to the Lenox police again, Kate. I mean, wow! We actually know what happened at the Gardner in 1990, which is a huge, huge deal. To just sit on this information could be – I mean, could what we're doing actually be illegal? Or if not tell the local cops, then maybe the FBI?"

She'd been slouching in her chair and now she sat up. "I know. I've actually been wondering about that. But, really, Timmy, then might not somebody else lay claim to the reward? The Lenox cops? The Federal Government? I mean, Aunt Mary confessed to *me* about the Gardner paintings, and if somehow they actually get returned to the museum intact, shouldn't *I* get the reward? And of course half for you, Donald. Don't worry, I'm not forgetting that."

"It hadn't slipped my mind, either."

"Well, you would have initiated the recovery," Timmy said. "And provided the crucial information. I'm just thinking about covering all our bases, legally speaking."

"There are two problems with that," I said. "I know that in similar situations, Timothy, you have thought of me as an anarchist in need of reining in. And on rare occasions, I admit that you might have been right. But this time the problems with your argument are more practical. One is, all of our reliable-sounding information has come from just one source, and that is the famous local criminal Fess Tetlow. I somehow can't picture the Lenox Police Department hauling Fess in, and when he denies ever saying all the things he revealed to me about the Gardner heist, they attach electrodes to his genitals to make him talk."

It's true," Kate said, "that in Lenox that approach would be considered in questionable taste."

"The other thing is, we aren't anywhere near actually having the missing art treasures in hand. For all we know, whoever has them now might have panicked and destroyed the lot of them. Or if the great art hasn't been destroyed yet, it could still get trashed if whoever has it sees the fuzz closing in."

Timmy, better read than I'll ever be, added to that, undercutting his own original argument. "I know there was a case in Europe where an art thief's mother burned some stolen masterpieces in her fireplace, in order, she believed, to protect her son."

"It sounds," I said, "as if the art ended up in Aunt Mary's living room after the heist mastermind died unexpectedly and the actual perpetrators panicked. We don't need any more panicked disposal of the art before it is safely in our richly-deserving-of-the-reward clutches."

Then, still more good luck. Kate's editor friend, Greg, at the *Eagle* phoned. He said he couldn't talk for long, but she should check her email. Greg said he'd turned up just one reference to Miles Tate in his LexisNexis search, and that was in a Boston Globe obituary for Monmouth Khachaturian. Strangely, Greg said, Tate otherwise did not seem even to exist.

Kate thanked her friend and eagerly fired up her laptop. And there it was in the March 22, 1990 *Globe*. She recited:

"The headline is 'Monmouth Khachaturian, 67, dies.' The news story reads: 'Well-known Newberry Street art gallery owner Monmouth Khachaturian died suddenly on Thursday of an apparent heart attack. Miles Tate, who identified himself as Khachaturian's assistant, said the respected specialist in classical European paintings collapsed in his office. EMT personnel responded but were unable to revive the art aficionado.

"'Tate said Khachaturian had been thought to be in good health and was looking forward to a business trip to Philadelphia the next day.

"'A native of Uzbekistan, Khachaturian came to the United States as a child and grew up in Milwaukee, where his late father, Gravlaw Khachaturian, was in the import business, and his mother, the former Nadya Aungst, was a homemaker. Khachaturian is survived by a sister, Della Vicknicki, of Concord. The future of the Khachaturian Gallery, Tate said, remains uncertain at this time.'"

We sat looking at each other. In the unusual brief silence, Arthur glanced over from the microwave to see if we were still alive and capable of opening doors.

Timmy said, "Business trip to Philadelphia. Hmm. The FBI suspected mobsters down there were somehow involved."

Kate said, "And Concord. Catchy's sister lived in Concord. Where Bucky is now. Or was a little while ago."

I checked my Spy-oh-my app. "And he's still there."

"It's seven-forty-five," Timmy said. "I wonder if he's spending the night."

"It's not all that far from Belmont, where I think he lives. So he could well be headed home for the night."

"Wait," Kate said, "I picked up Aunt Mary's belongings from Mount Mercy and I think I saw her address book there. I mean actual address book made out of paper. A device that would not give her brain cancer if she used it."

Kate got up and went into the cluttered little office she had just off the entrance to the B&B's dining room. She soon returned with a small address book with images of zinnias, probably uncut, on the cover.

"Here's where Bucky and Janice live. It's 211 Pratt Street, Belmont."

I made a note on my phone, probably a far less reliable

device for recording information than Mary Costello's card-board-and-paper Hallmark address book.

"Anyway," Timmy said, "didn't Janice the girlfriend say he wasn't coming home for a while?"

"And yet," Kate said, "he's not all that far away in Concord. Which is probably a ten-minute drive from Belmont."

We sat puzzling over that one when Kate's phone twittered again. She answered it and said things like "oh," "hmmm," "gee," and "oh, how interesting."

"You won't believe this," Kate said when she hung up.

Timmy said, "I'll bet we will."

"Melissa's friend in Boston remembers the Khachaturi-an Gallery very well. It closed soon after his sudden death. There were rumors at the time of art that was in the gallery disappearing before his heir, his sister Della, could take an inventory and include the art in the estate. The sister accused Khachaturian's mistress, an Elsa Gelman, of making off with all kinds of valuable paintings, which Gelman denied. This was also the time when Miles Tate left the gallery, which the sister was about to shut down, and left Boston. Melissa's friend said Tate told people he was moving west. He also said he was tired of the art world, which had become too cutthroat for his tastes. Instead, Tate planned on a total withdrawal from the life he was living at that time. He told friends he was going to take up a religious vocation."

CHAPTER 12

KATE INVITED US TO SPEND the night at the B&B, and I said great. Timmy was hesitant. He explained that he hadn't brought toiletries or clean clothes. Kate said she had extra toothbrushes and tooth paste on hand. She even offered to get up early and launder Timmy's clothing before he arose. "I remember," she said, "how in India you had a lower-caste woman who came every other day to wallop the dirt out of your clothes down by the river. It would be easier for me, what with this contraption-thing I have in the basement called a washing machine."

Peace Corps people didn't like to be reminded of their servants, I'd noticed over the years, and Timmy changed the subject and said he thought he could adapt to wearing the same clothes for a second day this one time.

Now we could kick back in Kate's cozy living room with its nice mixture of comfortable chairs and a long, low couch. The art in the room was mostly Asian, Buddha figures and Hindu gods and goddesses. I sat across from a large poster of Ganesh, the elephant-headed god with four arms and hands, who Kate said was a "remover of obstacles." I kept sending him silent messages: *Help us out here, Sir. Yes, we want the ten mil, but this thing is far bigger than mere gelt.*

"So, what do we think?" Timmy wondered. He and Kate had hit the chardonnay again and were doing what they could to mellow out despite all the unsolved puzzles we faced. "Miles Tate took up a religious vocation, so-called. Is he Father Mike Thigpen?"

"It seems like more than funny coincidence," Kate said, "that this guy hears Aunt Mary's confession about the Gardner art and then vanishes from view for – Donald, how long did the rectory say?"

"They told me ten days. A retreat, the guy who answered the phone said, somewhere in Vermont. Tomorrow I'll try to find out more. And maybe take a drive up north and ask Father Mike some pointed questions."

"He'll probably claim seal of the confessional," Timmy said. "The sacramental seal overrides everything, and common law generally supports that."

I almost replied, "But what if I broke his nose?" Instead, I said, "The threat of prosecution might loosen the guy's tongue. Priests can be sent to prison, as we have witnessed on numerous occasions in recent years."

"It still doesn't make sense," Timmy said. "Why would this man steal the art for any reason other than to return it to the Gardner? And if that had happened, it would have been breaking news all over the Northeast. What else was he going to do with the paintings? Fence them and donate the proceeds to the Archdiocese? The more I think about that, the crazier it sounds. The Archbishop wouldn't be able to explain to the Vatican where all the bushels of cash suddenly came from, since the church in the U.S. has been crying poverty for years."

"That would be odd," Kate agreed.

"Though if Father Thigpen *is* Miles Tate," Timmy said, "we're one up on Bucky. Knowing this puts us much closer to the stolen art than he is."

"And," I added, "it also gives us leverage over Bucky. If and when the time comes, we can maybe trade information."

Kate looked up from the wine glass she'd just re-half-filled. "Oh, I don't know about negotiating anything with Bucky. Rational discourse has never been his forte."

"Anyway," I said, "the whole priest-as-a-crook scenario just doesn't smell right to me, either. Kate, your friend said Tate told people he was heading west. That could have been the Berkshires, sure. Or it could have meant Wyoming. Or even farther. Bali? Thailand? The religious vocation, so-called, wouldn't necessarily have been Christian. The guy could have become a Buddhist monk, for all we know."

"East Asia is not west," Timmy murmured. He was stretched out on the couch and looking quite bleary-eyed. "You go west to get there, but it's really east by most geographical definitions."

"Such a useful piece of information," I said.

Kate stifled a yawn. "We're all tired. Maybe we should call it a night. Look at Arthur over there on his favorite chair. I think maybe he has the right idea."

"Your cat has that same idea about twenty-three and a half hours a day," I pointed out. "There must be a lot of care-free birds and mice in this neighborhood."

Kate looked as if she was about to gather herself up from her chair, but then she thought of something and stopped. "We're fixated on this runaway priest. But what about Bucky showing up in Concord, where Monmouth Khachaturian's sister lived. Is *that* also just coincidence?"

Timmy had struggled to a sitting position and was beginning to re-focus. "Maybe no coincidence, but it was thirty years ago she lived there. And if this Della Vicknicki was anywhere near Catchy's age, she'd be well into her nineties by now – if she's alive at all. So that feels like a stretch."

We all got out our phones, and I got the first hit, a feature story in *The Concord Journal* dated just a few months earlier. Della Vicknicki had just celebrated her ninety-fifth birthday with an open house at the art gallery she owned on Main Street in Concord. The gallery, called Della Fine Art, had been a mainstay on the local art scene, the story said, since – this was especially interesting – the year 1990.

CHAPTER 13

BEFORE I LEFT FOR Concord in the morning – its website said Della Fine Art would open at ten – I phoned the Pittsfield rectory again and reached a Father Moyer. I told him I needed to contact Father Mike Thigpen regarding a personal matter about which the priest had been counselling me.

"Father Mike is on a retreat," the cleric said, "and I'm not sure he's reachable at the present time. Perhaps I could be of help. What is the nature of your personal matter, Mr. Stacy?"

"Strachey. Donald. Doesn't Father Mike have a cell phone?"

"Yes, of course. But I have to tell you that when he left town a few days ago Father Mike was very clear that he did not wish to be disturbed. I'm sorry I really can't put you in touch. But if you wouldn't mind speaking with another counsellor, I'd be glad to be of help."

"Gosh, how long will Father Mike be gone?"

"About ten days. May I ask if you'll be all right waiting that long?"

"So, he's in Vermont? Yesterday somebody said Vermont. I mean, I could get somebody to drive me up there."

A little silence. "Where are you now, Donald?"

"I'm staying for the time being in Lenox. Where in Vermont is Father Mike staying? The southern part of the state, or way up?"

"Are you a resident at the Mount Mercy Care Facility, Donald? I know Father Thigpen provides spiritual counselling at Mount Mercy on a regular basis. Is that where you're in residence?"

"Yes, it is. In fact, he was here at the facility just this past Sunday. Did he mention anything about that particular visit to you or to any of the other priests, by chance?"

Another pause. Did this guy know something? "I don't recall that he did. Donald, may I ask about your health? Is that it? Are you seriously ill? How are you doing?"

Should I tell him I was sinking, and I doubted if I was going to last for ten days? No. Anyway, Timmy was seated nearby at Kate's kitchen table listening to my end of the conversation, and he might have objected. He was no longer much of a Catholic, but he would have drawn the line at playing mean games with a well-meaning man of God – if that's what Father Moyer was.

I said, "My health is poor, but I still get around with a little help from my friends. Now, let me ask you this, Father. After Father Mike visited Mount Mercy on Sunday, did he mention anything to you or others about some valuable paintings that had been stolen from a Boston museum thirty-some years ago? And how those paintings have suddenly resurfaced? Does any of that ring a bell?"

Now it was a much longer pause. Then, coolly: "Who are you, really? What the fuck is going on here? What game are you playing?"

"What game am *I* playing? The more important question is, what game is Father Thigpen playing? Maybe you could clue me in, Father, as to what this man-on-the-run is up to. There is an awful lot at stake here, and I am rapidly beginning to believe you know exactly what it is."

"I don't know who you really are, buddy, although I have my strong suspicions. Donald Strachey sounds to me like a fake name. One thing I do know is that we have nothing else to say to each other, and I am going to hang up and go back to finishing my breakfast. And don't call the rectory again, is my strong advice. Am I making myself clear?"

"You all are making a big mistake," I said, but midway in the sentence, the line went dead.

When I filled Timmy in on the conversation he'd only heard my half of, he said, "Bucky. The guy thinks you're Bucky."

"That's what I think he thinks, too."

"So maybe Father Thigpen *is* Miles Tate."

"Possibly. Though an entire Catholic rectory full of art thieves? I seriously doubt that."

"And the Rembrandts and the Vermeer are at this moment speeding their way to the Vatican? No, I don't think so, either. Anyway, the Vatican prefers sixteenth century Italian art to seventeenth century Dutch."

"Well, we're not going to call the FBI or the Diocese until we have a clearer picture of whether or not Father Mike is Miles Tate and exactly what this guy is up to. Maybe Catchy's sister Della can help us comprehend who Tate was and what became of him after the Khachaturian Gallery closed. She was there at the time and was involved in it all."

"Though she's ninety-five years old," Timmy reminded me. "I hope she doesn't have any memory problems."

CHAPTER 14

"NILES TATRO? OH, SURE, I remember him very well," Della Vicknicki croaked out. "Wasn't he the weatherman on Channel Five? Jean and I watched that every night at eleven for years and years. But I have to say, I never knew the man personally."

We were in her small office in the back of her gallery on Main Street in Concord. Della's own assistant, Solange something, a young woman dressed in black with long, straight hair, was minding the store out front.

"It's actually *Miles Tate* I'm interested in," I said loudly and clearly enough to make myself understood, I hoped, but not so loud that I appeared frustrated by the old lady's hearing difficulties. "I'm trying to track Tate down on behalf of a long-ago acquaintance."

She was a small bundle of human parts seemingly held together by an assortment of ropes, belts, and garments that looked as if she'd gotten into them when cold weather had set in the previous fall, and she hadn't quite gotten around to shedding this comfy get-up even as early summer approached. Her galvanized-bucket-colored hair was held in place by a white plastic barrette, and the ridges and valleys of her face contained a broad mouth with a continuous faint smile and two grey eyes that stayed well focused for a person of Ms. Vicknicki's vintage.

"Oh, Miles *Tate,* oh, yes, that's right. He was Monmouth's assistant at the gallery in Boston. Yes, I remember Miles Tate. He left town to become a monk or something. And how very odd your asking, Ronald. Another man came in just before we closed the shop yesterday afternoon and was asking the very same thing, did I know where Miles Tate was?"

"Who was that inquirer, if I may ask?"

"Walter something. Was it Walter? Yes, I think it was. Or if not Walter, some other name starting with a W. Or maybe a Y. But I told the man I simply had no idea where Miles Tate would be, I hadn't had contact with Tate for over thirty years. This Walter – he had a Red Sox cap on that he never took off – this man was actually rather rude. When I said I was sorry not to be able to help him out, he turned around and tramped out the door with nary a thank you nor a by-your-leave. Is he someone you know, or know of, Ron?"

"I don't know him, but I know of him. His name is Walter. I'm not surprised he was impolite."

"Miles Tate seems to be awfully popular all of a sudden. What's that about?"

"The thing is," I said, "Mr. Tate may possess some valuable objects that do not belong to him."

"Oh, dear."

"You mentioned, Della, that Tate may have left Boston in order to become a monk. What kind of monk?"

"Oh, I couldn't say. It was just something I heard. I barely knew the man. Jean always thought there was something fishy about him. But Monmouth trusted the young fellow, so at the time I supposed he was all right. He certainly knew French and Dutch art. But now you're saying people think he was dishonest? That's a bit unsettling. Maybe Jean was onto something. She was a good judge of people."

"Jean was your business partner? Or were you not in business in 1990?"

We were both drinking tea from old WBUR public radio mugs. Della had fortified hers with clotted milk , India-style, like Timmy.

"Girlfriend," she said with a wink. "Nowadays they say partner. Or wife even. We were together for sixty-two years, lucky us. Way back when, I was married to Mr. Vicknicki for a short time, but that didn't go so well. Jean died three years ago, way before Covid. She had a stroke weeding in the garden, and off she went. She was always business-like – she was an insurance broker – and keeling over dead with no fuss at all was Jean all the way."

"Was Jean your age? I read in the Concord Journal that you're an enviable ninety-five."

"She was ten years younger. That's what's so baffling and annoying about the whole thing, her careening off to oblivion so much sooner than me. Do you really envy my being ninety-five? I'll be glad to trade places with you, Ron."

"Enviable was the wrong word. Impressed, I should have said."

"You might not have noticed, but my hearing is awful. I've got my marbles, though. And my heart is good, Mary Jane says. She's my doctor. I'm lucky to have a strong heart. It's how my brother died, you know. A heart attack that came out of nowhere. The man had hardly been sick a day in his life. And then, ka-bang! We were all just stunned."

"What a shock it must have been."

"Monmouth and I weren't all that close. He had his life in town, and I had mine out here. Though I *was* his heir. He had his various lady friends over the years, but those rarely lasted more than a year or two, and at least he knew better than to put any of those women in his will. A bunch of gold-diggers, Jean always said. I was a pretty lucky sister in that regard. Up to a point, anyhow."

"Up to a point?"

An apologetic toss of her aged head. "Do you really want to hear all this Khachaturian family mishigas from years and years and years ago? It's all chickens over the dam by now. I'm not sure I really care anymore, and I can't imagine that anybody else does."

"I read that you opened your gallery here in Concord in

1990. Did your brother leave you the inventory of his New-berry Street business? Or were there complications, and that's what you meant by being a lucky heiress *up to a point*?"

"You guessed it," she said, giving me a sour look. "You said you were a detective, and I kind of wish you'd been around back then, because I could have used an Inspector Maigret."

"I'd like to have been there."

"There was surprisingly little in the way of cash or securities in Monmouth's estate. There were rumors of large sums in numbered Swiss accounts, and in the Cayman Islands. But I was never able to track any of that down, so maybe it wasn't really true. What there was, though, were a lot of valuable paintings in Monmouth's gallery. Mostly Dutch, Flemish and French, seventeenth century. But when I went with an appraiser the day after Monmouth's funeral, most of it had disappeared. Just gone up in smoke. Fortunately, a number of choice pieces of work were still there. That's what made it possible for me to open this place. But hundreds of thousands of dollars' worth of work was missing, according to some collectors I knew who had visited the gallery in recent weeks. And do you know what, Ronald? I knew exactly who the likely thief was."

"Who?"

"Elsa Gelman."

I'd heard this story from Kate's friend's friend, but I said, "Who was that?"

Her hand trembled as she lifted her public radio mug for a sip of tea. "Elsa had been Monmouth's mistress for almost three years, and she claimed he had told her she was his rightful heiress, and he was about to change his will. Monmouth's lawyer told me he knew nothing about this, and I'm sure the woman was lying through her fake teeth."

"She...she wore dentures?"

"I've heard some men find that useful."

This was a topic I wished to hear no more about. "So you think she believed the art in the gallery was rightfully hers, and she took it?"

"Only three people had a key to my brother's gallery, the insurance company told Hal Bloom, Monmouth's attorney. And one of them was Elsa. She had no gallery, but she dealt in European art and she had a clientele of her own. For months afterwards, I tried to keep tabs on her sales to see what might turn up. But Elsa was a slippery character, and I never got the goods on her, I'm sorry to say."

"*Was* a slippery character? Is she no longer living?"

"Elsa died in a Green Line crash in Brookline about ten years ago. I heard she had been living quite comfortably in a big house on Summit Avenue. Where she came up with the wherewithal to live the way she did, I can't say for sure. But I think I can guess."

This all sounded plausible enough. But of course I had another idea. I said, "Elsa Gelman had one key to your brother's gallery. Who had the other two?"

"Well, Monmouth, naturally. And of course his assistant, Miles Tate." She blinked. "So, what are you hinting at, Ronald? Do you think it might have been Miles who opened the door to the gallery one night and walked off with a over a million dollars' worth of paintings?"

"There are those of us who suspect that that might be the case."

Ms. Vicknicki looked suddenly aghast. "If that's true," she said, "then for years Monmouth would have had a dishonest man working in his employ. How awful to learn that. And to think that Monmouth never suspected a thing!"

CHAPTER 15

I WASN'T ABOUT TO BE the one to break the news to Della Vicknicki that her late brother was a major crook. Not only that, but he was the crook behind what was probably the most notorious art theft in history not carried out by a colonial power. I did ask her if perhaps a fourth key to the Khachaturian gallery might have been hidden somewhere – probably not under a rock on busy Newberry Street – but she doubted that would have been the case.

So, like Bucky, I was back to Miles Tate. The only thing about Tate's departure from the never-to-reopen gallery Ms. Vicknicki could remember was a phone call from him expressing condolences over her brother's passing. It was Tate's expressed opinion that it must have been the stress of the art world "rat race" that led to the dealer's heart attack. So Ms. Vicknicki wasn't surprised, she said, when acquaintances on Newberry Street told her soon after that Tate had left Boston on some type of spiritual quest. Who were these acquaintances of thirty years earlier? She did recall a few names, but all of these people had since "bit the dust," she said.

It would have been nice to stroll around Concord, a prosperous-looking town where the first shots in the American revolution were fired and where later Ralph Waldo Emerson and the Alcotts raised a commotion that was explosive in its more sedate literary way. But with Mary Costello's funeral just two days away and the fate of the Gardner art still a mystery, I badly needed to get back to Lenox.

From outside a Concord Starbucks where I competed in Timmy's tiny Honda with highly caffeinated oldsters in Mini Coopers and gigantic Volvos for the limited parking spaces available, I checked my Spy-oh-my for Bucky's current location. I was very much interested to see that he was actually in Boston, only twenty-some miles away from where I sat enjoying a mocha Frappuccino. He was on the move, however, in a heavy-traffic area of the South End. So there seemed no point in making my way over there, inasmuch as my device would only lead me to Bucky's general vicinity, and Kate had told me she had no idea what kind of vehicle Bucky was currently driving. I should have asked Fess Tetlow about that and planned on doing so if I could locate him a second time at *No Trespassing Asshole* back in Glendale.

Next, I phoned Timmy back at Kate's house. He said no news was no news. Kate had spoken with the other two Garden Club members who possessed keys to Aunt Mary's house, Carla Mariori and Peg Williamson, and Kate was convinced that neither was a likely candidate for having stolen the art treasures from behind the cow painting. Both women planned on attending the Saturday funeral, where we could check them out additionally.

I described my visit with Della Vicknicki and told Timmy how Bucky had apparently been there the day before as part of his own search for Miles Tate. And that he had left the Vicknicki gallery as uninformed as I was. I said to Timmy that Bucky was back in Boston, and what might that mean? That he had tracked Miles Tate to somewhere in the South End? And if so, what about the possibly-formerly-Miles-Tate Father Thigpen? He was in far off Vermont – or so I had been told. It was confusing.

Timmy had a theory. "Tetlow did say that Bucky somehow had the phone number of the mystery man that Bucky thinks has the Gardner paintings. So maybe he's tracking Tate the same way you're tracking him."

"I did think of that, but I'm wondering about this: if the mystery man is Tate, how would Bucky even know the guy's phone number after all these years?"

"Good question. Would Tate even have the same phone number thirty years later? Hardly anybody does. Just some people's grandmothers, I think."

"It's puzzling. Anyway, I'm heading back to Lenox and will see you in a couple of hours. How's Kate doing? She was pretty stressed after I left this morning. She seemed convinced that Father Thigpen is a thief and has absconded to Vermont and maybe handed over the Rembrandts and the Vermeer to the Archdiocese up there, or maybe the Bernie Sanders campaign."

After a moment, Timmy said quietly – maybe Kate was within earshot – that she had another bad headache and she wasn't feeling well at all.

"In fact," Timmy said, "a very upsetting thing happened a while ago. You know that the funeral home in Pittsfield had asked her for a deposit on the funeral after Bucky told them he was broke, and she gave them her credit card information."

I said I did remember that.

"Well, the credit card was declined. Kate thought she had a few thousand in credit left. But she had forgotten she used Visa to pay for a major repair job on her oil burner that she'd been told was necessary if she wanted to continue to have hot water come out of her taps. So that came as a rude surprise. Well, worse than rude."

"Damn. So what did she do? With funerals, you can't sort of improvise or fake it."

I could hear his deep breath. "I gave her my MasterCard to use. No need for you to worry. I'm not. She'll pay me back when she can, I have absolutely no doubt at all."

"Timothy, you are a true friend," I said. "Maybe Kate will even give *you* a cut of the ten mil that's soon coming her way."

He chuckled briefly.

CHAPTER 16

I WAS BACK IN LENOX by 1:30 and filled Timmy in additionally on my Concord excursion. He had called his office at the State Capitol in Albany and had told his boss, Assemblyman Myron Lipschitz, that he wouldn't be in for the rest of the week. This was not a problem, as hard-working and reliable Timmy had accumulated plenty of leave time.

Anyway, the state budget had been completed in May, only a month late, and the Legislature was preoccupied with an alleged-sexual-harassment scandal involving the state's handsy governor, Andrew Cuomo. New legislation, Timmy's area of expertise, was the last thing on anybody's mind in Albany.

Kate had gone upstairs to lie down for a while, but during the morning she had talked to her contacts at *The Berkshire Eagle*. She had obtained some dope on Bucky Costello's history of law-breaking, which Timmy summarized in his customary clear and organized way. There actually wasn't much, since Bucky's records as a juvenile law-breaker had been appropriately sealed. But two things were of interest. Bucky had two assault convictions going back to 1989, and each time he had spent a month in the Suffolk County – that's Boston – lock-up.

What was this? Kate had told me that all of Bucky's run-ins with the law involved non-violent infractions and she

93

couldn't imagine him actually hurting another person. And yet, here were actual jailable violent offenses. No details of these incidents were readily available, but I figured I really ought to chase them down.

Kate had requested any information the *Eagle* had in its files on Father Mike Thigpen, and the one item the paper supplied was a profile of the priest when he'd arrived in Pittsfield five years earlier to become the parish priest at St. Margaret's Church. The report said that previously he had served similarly in Holyoke and before that in Fall River. There was no mention of where the pastor had grown up or anything at all about his earlier life. Did that absence mean anything, or did the brevity of the story simply indicate its limited newsworthiness?

The profile was accompanied by a photo of the clergyman. He was a good-looking, curly-headed man of fifty or so – a plausible age for Miles Tate five years earlier – with what some people would call a sly smile. He also appeared to have a well-preserved physique for a man his age.

Timmy sent the photo to me, and I forwarded it to Della Vicknicki with a note asking her if this man looked at all like Miles Tate.

Timmy and I were seated on Kate's side porch enjoying the Macy's-perfume-counter, almost-too-sweet aroma of the lilacs. The sky had begun to cloud over – the forecast was for a chance of scattered showers. Arthur was reclining on his milk crate apparently waiting patiently for us to make any interesting moves.

I was about to head down to Fess Tetlow's cannabis trap house when a text arrived from Laurel Peaseley at Strathmore Investigations. She asked me if I had made any decision as to my going to work for Strathmore. She said other applicants for the job were standing by, but I was certainly "still number one in the queue."

I said, "What a pest this woman is. What a royal pain in the ass. What a noodge. Why, Timothy, she's – she's just like *me!*"

"It does sound as if you'd fit right in there."

"You bet I would. Pester the fuck out of people until you get whatever it is you want out of them. Is that yours truly, or is that not yours truly?"

He sniffed. "But they did say previously that you had until Friday to let them know. What this woman is doing is beyond assertive. It's rude."

"I love," I said, "her saying I was *still* number one in the queue. I haven't slipped to, say, number twelve."

"One term you could use to describe Ms. Peaseley is passive-aggressive."

"It's an approach that often works, too. I use it frequently."

He laughed. "I've noticed."

Surely he was kidding. "The question is, can I afford to continue being a royal-pain independent operator, or must I admit that the world is changing and I have to change with it? Because of Covid, and because of the efficiencies as well as the ruthlessness of the big operators, small businesses are disappearing faster than the trees in the world's rainforests are. Can I still get away with being Phillip Marlowe – with the occasional Micky Spillane thrown in – or do I have to accept that AT&T and Amazon are the future, and I have to hook up with the behemoths if I'm going to have any future at all as an investigator? As a great king once said, Is a puzzlement."

"King Mongkut never actually said that," Timmy pointed out. "Just Yul Brenner."

Timmy and I had traveled to Thailand a number of times, and he had of course boned up on the country's history. I had been mainly interested in the spicy green papaya salad and the massage parlors.

"So, what to do? Anyway, I really do have another twenty-four hours to decide. And maybe we'll find the lost Gardner masterpieces in the meantime and my five mil cut of the reward will settle everything, no?"

"Sounds good to me," Timmy said, knowing exactly what I was likely to do, no matter what.

Then an email came in that put a damper on any of that. Della Vicknicki wrote: "Dear Ron, I saw the photo you sent. That doesn't look at all like Miles Tate. Who is that priest-looking fellow meant to be, anyway?"

CHAPTER 17

"YEAH, THAT'S THAT ASS-WIPE, Miles Tate," Tetlow muttered. "The priest get-up throws me off a little bit, but that's probably him. I mean, holy fuck, what's he doing in that outfit? Is he really a pastor now? He's older, also, in this picture, and he has more hair on his head, but if I had to say for sure, I'd say that might be him."

Tetlow was sucking in a few of nature's more playful chemicals from another blunt, this one the size of my forearm. Recreational weed was now legal in the Commonwealth of Massachusetts, and you could just go down to your friendly neighborhood pot shop and stock up on cannabis the way you might pop into Walgreens for glue sticks or vitamin B-12. Tetlow had apparently done just that, and it wasn't gummies or brownies for this stoner's stoner, it was your Uncle Huck's reefer, the entire hippie-dippy-days-of-yore-bring-a-smile-to-your-face sooty chimney.

And, again, as we stood in the *No Trespassing Asshole* driveway, I inhaled some of Fess's forget-your-troubles nice fumes.

"So, you think this picture *might* be Miles Tate, but you aren't sure?"

"It's him, all right. I'm pretty sure. But the disguise is confusing me."

"This guy is an actual priest. Before Tate left Boston, he

told people he planned on leading a more spiritual life. So it's possible he changed his identity and actually studied for the priesthood and was ordained."

Tetlow kept squinting down at the image on my phone, but he was having trouble focusing and I didn't need to wonder why. "I suppose it's a good cover," he said. "Most of those Catholic dudes are phonies, anyhow. They're all wine-drinking alkies. My folks went to the Methodist church. They only drank Sprite and gin."

When he seemed to have no additional point to make, I said, "I take it Bucky hasn't been in touch with you since he was here on Monday. Or has he?"

Tetlow made a face and said something like, *Pfooof*. Then: "No, and if he came around again and I saw him coming I'd haul my ass out of here. The next time he came, I'd be afraid Bucky'd bring his baseball bat along. I don't think he'd go off on me especially, but with that dude you just never know."

Here it was again. "Bucky can be violent?"

Another casual toke. "Mostly, no, Bucky's way cool. But once in while…. And then, look out!"

"I know he did some jail time in 1989 in Boston for assault. Is that the kind of thing you're referring to?"

Tetlow leaned against Timmy's car and struggled to look grave. "I was there for one of those deals. Bucky thought some stupid jerk was walking out of his apartment with a couple of his baseball cards. Bucky went after the guy with his Ted Williams bat he usually keeps with him, and this doofus ends up in Boston City for a week. The bastard was lucky Bucky didn't kill him. Another time – I wasn't there for this one – Bucky thought some drunk guy at a party insulted his mom. It was totally ridiculous! This dude didn't even know Bucky's mom, who lived way out here in Lenox. But Bucky thinks he hears a certain thing, and out comes the Ted Williams bat all over again. Both of those guys called the cops on him, and Bucky was lucky he didn't end up in Walpole. There were other times, too, I heard, but by then I was back here helping out Ma, who was looking after Dad. He'd come down with tongue cancer. Christ Almighty, don't ever get that one, Donald. I mean, Jesus."

"Yeah, that sounds like the worst. I guess I'll have to be careful when I locate Bucky," I added, and I meant it.

I asked Tetlow what kind of car Bucky was driving when he'd shown up in Glendale on Monday, and if the car was his.

"I suppose it was his car, an old red Hyundai with a lot of Sox stickers on the bumpers and rear end. Yeah, be careful if you cross paths with the Buckster. Most of the time you wouldn't want to meet a nicer guy. But now that he's all rip-shit over those museum pictures, you probably don't want to mess with him. Good luck finding the pictures. And if you find Miles Tate, give the asshole a wedgie from me."

"I will."

"A wedgie, but not a kiss."

"What do you mean?"

"Bucky and I were sure the guy was a faggot. Bucky said, Just so he doesn't try anything with me and him. And Bucky meant it. I'm sure he would've gone after the guy with his bat."

CHAPTER 18

"SO NOW DO WE THINK Tate was gay?" Timmy asked. "Or is this just Bucky and Fess assuming anybody less butch than Hannibal Lecter is a big swish?"

"I tried to get Fess to elaborate on his and Bucky's idea that Tate was one of our people, but I didn't get anywhere. The fact that Tate went around in anything other than a Sox cap on backwards and a hairy belly hanging out between his belt and his Bud-lite T-shirt might have been enough to nail the guy as a perv. But who knows? I didn't, needless to say, take umbrage at Tetlow's use of the term *faggot*, and announce, 'See here, my good fellow, I happen to be one of those, too!' I might need to talk to the fuck-head again."

"The most interesting thing you told us," Kate said, "was Fess saying Bucky could be violent. I have to say I'm surprised. I just never, ever saw anything like that."

"Yes, usually there are early signs," Timmy put in. "Bullying or throwing rocks at the other kids or torturing animals."

At the word *animals*, Arthur looked up briefly. We were back on Kate's porch waiting for Father Steven Sondergaard to arrive. He was the St. Agnes parish priest who would deliver the eulogy for Mary Costello on Saturday, and he wished to gather some family anecdotes to include in his remarks. A light rain had begun to fall, which was no surprise, as it had been an unusually wet spring. Hank Thurmer had said this weather was "good for the rhubarb," and who were we to dispute that?

"If Bucky is that volatile," I said, "I think we have to assume he could be very dangerous when we finally catch up with him. The fact that he actually took time off from his beloved job at Fenway is one indication of the state he's in."

"If I was chasing half a billion dollars' worth of art that I thought somebody had filched from me," Timmy said, "I'd be tetchy, too."

"Though you don't have a history of going after people with a baseball bat. That's one way you and Bucky are different."

"One of several."

"Of course," Kate reminded us, "there are lots of gay people in the art world. It doesn't sound as if Monmouth Khachaturian was, but people who worked for him could easily have been. It's hardly a baseless stereotype."

Timmy raised an eyebrow. "And if Tate was gay, and now he's Father Thigpen – oh my goodness!"

"Yes, a gay priest. Who ever heard of such a thing?"

"Now this is starting to add up," Timmy mused. "Or is it? It's still awfully confusing. The possibilities seem all but endless. So, Don. What does your gadget say? Is Bucky still in Boston?"

I checked my Spy-oh-my. "He is. He's no longer in the South End, though. Now he's in Back Bay, not far from Fenway Park. I guess if the Red Sox are his religion, Bucky is constantly hearing the call of the Mother Church. He just can't stay away."

"But," Kate said, "he told the Sox management he'd be away from work all week. If he's at the park, what's he doing there?"

"It's tempting," I said, "to drive out there. It would take a couple of hours. The thing is, Bucky seems to be constantly on the move. If he's indoors somewhere, I'd have a hard time zeroing in. If he's driving, it'd be easier, since Tetlow gave me a good description of Bucky's car with its Sox-sticker decorations. But he'd have to have his phone on just for me to get anywhere close by. And sometimes he turns the phone off."

We went back and forth for several minutes on whether or not I should risk driving across the state of Massachusetts for a second time that day with the hope I could get close enough to Bucky to actually spot him. And hope he wasn't carrying his Ted Williams baseball bat.

I was still trying to decide what to do when Father Sondergaard showed up, and by the time he left Kate's house an hour later I was very glad I had stuck around to hear what *he* had to say.

CHAPTER 19

"IT'S TRUE," THE PRIEST said, "that your aunt was a bit of an odd bird."

"Everybody knew that," Kate agreed, "but it didn't really matter to people. She was friendly and generous and considerate, and of course her flower garden was one of the wonders of Walker Street."

"I think a lot of people," Father Sondergaard went on, "found Mary Costello's eccentricities delightfully disarming. I know I did. And people in Lenox are generally so environmentally conscious that they don't mind if a particular brand of environmentalism is a bit off-beat."

We were still on Kate's porch, Timmy, Kate, and the pastor enjoying a glass of chardonnay, me with another Azerbaijani beer. Father Sondergaard, a stocky, open-faced man of sixty or so was not in priestly garb but in casual civies, khakis and a windbreaker.

"I think it would be fine," Kate said, "if you mention some of Aunt Mary's stranger beliefs in your remarks. There's no need to pretend she was anybody but who she was. Anyway, God knows Lenox is not lacking a sizeable population of eccentrics. She was just one of dozens. You must have more than a few of that particular type in the St. Agnes congregation."

"Oh, I suppose that's so." The pastor chuckled but plainly

wasn't going to head down that road.

"Some people might argue," Kate ventured on, "that there are more Congregationalists in town who are a little funny in the head than there are Catholics. But I'm guessing you're unlikely to have an opinion about that, Father."

He chuckled again, and said, "One thing I've sometimes wondered about, Kate. Your aunt believed that the flowers in her garden had souls of a kind and she refused ever to cut short their lives prematurely. But did she not eat vegetables? Were vegetables of a lower order, soul-wise?"

Kate grinned. "Aunt Mary not only ate vegetables, she also ate meat. At a family dinner many years ago, she served a leg of lamb that was absolutely scrumptious. And, as I recall, she did not eschew serving herself a nice portion after everyone else at the table had been taken care of."

"Where did she buy the lamb?" Timmy inquired. "When I lived in India, Buddhists never killed animals. But they bought meat from Muslim butchers and chowed down happily on that."

Kate didn't have to think that over. "I know Aunt Mary shopped at Lenox Price Chopper. And I doubt she knew the religion of the butchers there."

I said, "Mrs. Costello certainly liked cows. For many years she hung a painting she had done of cows in a field in South Williamstown on her living room wall. You probably saw it there, Father."

"I did, and I enjoyed looking at it. Mrs. Costello was certainly a competent amateur painter."

"It's very sad what happened to that painting. Have you heard about that?"

A puzzled look. "No, what happened?"

"Someone got into the house just after Mrs. Costello died and vandalized the painting. Nothing else was damaged, and we're all quite puzzled as to who might have done this and why."

He peered over at me with obvious concern. "What a ridiculous thing! And the police are investigating? How very odd."

Kate said, "The police are looking into it, supposedly. But it doesn't seem like a high priority."

The priest appeared truly surprised by this news, and I wasn't surprised by his surprise. Still, I asked him: "Was there any particular reason that Mount Mercy called a priest other than yourself to hear Mrs. Costello's confession on Sunday? Not that it matters a whole lot. But you had a history with Kate's aunt, and I wondered if the nursing home was remiss in failing to contact you. It surely would have meant something for Mrs. Costello to have the last rites administered by her parish priest."

Father Sondergaard gave me a mild who-is-this-guy? look. "Of course I would have been happy to hear this dear woman's confession. But I was out of town Sunday afternoon. In fact, I just returned to Lenox yesterday. I was off visiting my younger sister."

"No worry, it wasn't a problem," Kate said. "Mount Mercy has clergy they can always call."

"In fact," the priest said, "I learned of Mrs. Costello's passing from my secretary, who phoned me on Monday. Then I was contacted by the mortuary about funeral arrangements. I was surprised that the request was for a funeral Mass on Saturday – instead of Wednesday or Thursday, which would have been normal."

"I was surprised, too," Kate said.

"This was according to the wishes of Mrs. Costello's son Walter, I was told."

"Yes. His name is Walter, but he goes by Bucky."

"I have never met Bucky. And still have had no contact with him at all. McGonigal's told me he wanted the funeral service to be Saturday – something to do with obligations Bucky had at work in Boston – and there were to be no calling hours at the funeral home. And more unusual still, no graveside ceremony following the Mass. I was requested to be present for the burial, but no others were to be in attendance. I have to say, all this is – strange. Kate, have you any idea what's going on in young Mr. Costello's head?"

Kate rolled her eyes. "It's all somewhat murky at this point."

"Well, his mother had her peculiar ideas, and it sounds as if the son does, too."

"Yes, he is also eccentric."

"I understand your aunt is to be laid to rest in the Lee Catholic Cemetery next to her late husband. But you haven't been asked to attend?"

"I haven't, no. I have not actually been in touch with my cousin Bucky. He seems to have gone incommunicado."

The pastor furrowed his brow. "It sounds as if he is grief-stricken. Does he have access to spiritual counselling, that you know of?"

"I don't know about that. My impression is, Bucky has fallen away from the church. But we have not actually been in touch for years, so I can't say for sure."

Ever the diplomat, Father Sondergaard did not ask Kate why he had not spotted *her* in a St. Agnes pew since his arrival in Lenox some years earlier.

I helped him out by changing the subject. "With you out of town, Father, Mount Mercy was able to bring in Father Michael Thigpen from Pittsfield to hear Mrs. Costello's confession. He seems to be on some list of theirs and does counselling at the nursing home on a regular basis. Do you know him?"

He smiled. "Oh sure. Father Mike. I know him well. In fact, I ran into him just the other day. He didn't mention that Mary Costello had passed. It must have slipped his mind. But she was not one of his parishioners."

"Where did you see him? In Vermont?"

"Vermont? Oh no. I was with my sister Beverly having dinner at a Legal Seafoods in Boston, and in walked Father Mike and another priest. It was such a nice surprise."

CHAPTER 20

AMONG THE ANECDOTES Kate told Father Sondergaard for his eulogy was the one about her Aunt Mary tripping and falling during a late-afternoon walk up the Kennedy Park hill with her late husband, Lewis. Mrs. Costello was not injured, but a crown that had been recently installed on a tooth fell out.

The Costellos crawled around on the ground looking for the object, but they had no luck locating it. Soon, other walkers who happened by offered to help out. Within fifteen minutes, a dozen mostly elderly Lenox residents were on their hands and knees in search of the elusive dental appliance.

By chance, an Albany channel TV news van was nearby covering discovery of an embezzlement at the Lenox Savings Bank. And when someone told the reporter what was happening on Kennedy Park hill, she and her camera man hiked up the path to the spot and recorded the search. They were there when Eleanora Booksmith found the expensive crown under a fern and returned it to Mrs. Costello. It all made the 11 p.m. news on Channel 13, which a good number of people in Lenox were sure to tune in to.

"That's a wonderful story," Father Sondergaard said, grinning. "Just the sort of thing to lighten everybody's mood and show your aunt in all her humanity."

None of us piped up and said, "She also hid the Gardner Museum stolen Rembrandts and Vermeer behind the cow painting in her living room for over thirty years."

We did question the priest conversationally about his encountering Father Mike Thigpen at a Boston fish restaurant on Tuesday evening.

"He was in Boston?" I asked. "I think we heard he was in Vermont."

"Oh no. Maybe another time."

"On a retreat or something."

"Not this time, I don't think. No, this seemed to be a social occasion. Father Mike and a colleague."

I couldn't think of a way of asking who the *colleague* was without seeming strangely nosy, so I let that go.

"And Father Mike didn't mention Mary Costello's passing? Well, you clergy have so many occasions to usher the faithful into the beyond. Though I don't suppose it ever becomes routine."

"Not at all routine. Not ever, really. The occasion of any soul's passage of return to the Heavenly Father is unique and holy. That's always the case. With Covid, there *have* been times when some of us got a bit jammed up. The unexpected deaths just kept coming at us. But no administering of the final rites ever, ever feels routine."

Sondergaard gave me a look that said, Who is this clueless twit? and I supposed I had that coming – in his case and possibly others.

After Father Sondergaard headed back to his car with a copy of *The Berkshire Eagle* over his head against the rain, Kate said, "So. Father Thigpen. He seems to be an awfully long way from Vermont."

"Why," Timmy asked, "did the priest at the rectory in Pittsfield lie about Thigpen's whereabouts?"

"And," I added, "direct a profanity at me when I asked him about any knowledge the priest had of valuable art hidden in Mary Costello's living room?"

"These guys are up to their clerical collars in this thing," Timmy said. "It seems pretty obvious."

"But not Father Sondergaard," Kate said. "He seemed to

me to be oblivious to any treachery that might be underway."

Timmy laughed mirthlessly. "Yeah, unless he's the most cunning of them all."

I said, "He strikes me as sincere."

"Oh, Donald, Donald. You Presbyterians just don't know."

"People have told me that on prior occasions."

"Intrigue in the Church is as old as when Pope Stephen the Sixth had his predecessor Formosus disinterred and his corpse put on trial for blasphemy. And while *The Da Vinci Code* is mostly a crock, the parts about disinformation and cover-ups are all totally plausible and worthy of the Trump era."

"It's too bad," Kate said, "that we don't have Father Thigpen's phone number. And be able to see where he is the way we can with Bucky."

"And see if Bucky is closing in on him – if Bucky also thinks he's really Miles Tate. But," I pointed out, "the fact is, we don't have the priest's phone number. And nobody seems to want to tell us how to contact him."

Kate shook her head and shifted in her chair, which scraped an inch or so on the porch's wooden deck. Arthur eyed this development suspiciously, but only for a second or two.

I said, "The rectory won't give me any information. But, Kate, they might tell you. I mean, if you say you're Father Thigpen's sister and you need to reach the father on account of a family emergency."

She gave me the old Indian head wobble indicating ambivalence or maybe aversion. I was reminded that Timmy wasn't the only person to make this peculiar gesture. It was Timmy and 1.3 billion others on the Asian subcontinent, and now Kate Webster.

"I'm not sure I can do that," Kate said. "I'll start stuttering or something. Possibly even burst out laughing."

"Anyway," Timmy said, "why wouldn't Father Thigpen's sister already have his phone number?"

"All right, say cousin. And the cousin doesn't have the

phone number because – the sister had it, and she just died. That's it. Say his sister Martha has died unexpectedly."

Kate gave me a what-the-hell-kind-of-thing-are-you-saying? shake of the head. "Don, that's horrible. Are you really serious?"

Timmy rolled his eyes. "Oh, yes. He's serious."

Kate said, "God."

"Let me put it this way. If we can track down Father Thigpen and find out if he took the Gardner paintings and he has possession of them – and if we succeed at this before Bucky gets to Thigpen – there could well be ten million dollars in it for you, Kate. Ten million for you and of course for the others among us who are helping you out with this."

She sat silently for a long minute or two. Her eyes were closed, like Arthur's. And then she opened her eyes and picked up her phone.

CHAPTER 21

"SO, NOW WHAT?" KATE wondered aloud to Timmy and me. "They wouldn't give me Thigpen's phone number. The priest I talked to just said he'd pass the message to Father Thigpen and ask him to call me. I don't suppose I should hold my breath."

Timmy agreed. "Not if Father Thigpen doesn't have a sister named Martha."

"What if he *does* have a sister named Martha, and my call totally freaks the guy out? My God, I'd really hate doing that to him."

"But what are the odds he'd have a sister named Martha? I wouldn't worry too much about that."

"If Thigpen really is Miles Tate," I said, "it's possible he'll think the call was from somebody who Bucky put up to it. After I talked to that Father Moyer yesterday and all but accused Thigpen of stealing the Gardner paintings, he no doubt tipped off Thigpen that somebody was tracking him and that that somebody was probably Bucky."

"But now he'll have my phone number" Kate said. "And I don't have any kind of caller-ID blocking device. Uh oh."

"Even if Thigpen finds out it's you who's after him," I said, "so what? The guy has to be smart enough to know that once the paintings turned up missing from Mrs. Costello's living room, you'd have your suspicions about him. That would have been true with or without his ID-ing your call just now. But what is he going to do? Alert the FBI? Hardly. Or send a gang of thug seminarians on the payroll of the Springfield Diocese up to Lenox to rough you up? That's not likely, either."

Kate reached over to refill her wine glass and Arthur opened his eyes long enough to take note. "Father Thigpen must have some kind of way of blocking his identity from Bucky. If Bucky has his phone number, how come he can't find out who the owner of that number is?"

"There are services that will tell you who owns a cell number. You just sign up and pay a fee. But some subscribers pay to have their ID's blocked, and only law enforcement can penetrate that zone of privacy."

"And Bucky," Timmy said, "is not law enforcement. Just ask law enforcement."

"It's possible," I said, "that we are completely off base, and Father Thigpen isn't Miles Tate at all. And all the lying and covering up at the rectory have nothing to do with your aunt's confession and the stolen art treasures. But minus any other good ideas, the wily priest is still our best bet. For sure, the Lenox Garden Club ladies are far from convincing suspects."

"Or Hank Thurmer," Timmy said.

"Or doofus-y Fess Tetlow," Kate added.

"It's possible," I said, "that we're all missing the obvious here. That the culprit – or culprits – are all but in plain sight right here in Lenox, and they're people none us has ever heard of. The whole business of keys to the Costello house floating around town like apple blossoms on a breezy day opens up all kinds of possibilities. Likewise the house key under the rock. We have to stay alert to any evidence at all that someone other than Father Thigpen – or even the will-o'-the-wispy Miles Tate, should he not have become a Pittsfield parish priest – had both the means and the opportunity to get into the Costello house and make off with the poorly secured valuable art. For all we know, it could be just about anybody."

We all sat looking glum.

"All true," Timmy said.

"Oh, dear." I guessed Kate was thinking about her Visa account again.

"On the other hand, we know what we know. The good father is acting like a criminal on the run. He's in Boston – not Vermont – and so is Bucky. Bucky is constantly on the move, and so, apparently, is Father Thigpen."

"Do you mean he's on the move, so-called, because he ate in a restaurant?" Timmy queried.

"Don't they usually eat meals in a rectory?" was my lame reply.

"Maybe in the year 1170 they did. Nowadays, I think Catholic priests' dining habits vary quite a bit. Think of Albany," Timmy said, and mentioned an esteemed Italian restaurant down the hill from the Capitol on Grand Street.

"The thing is," I continued, reaching for firmer ground, "we could probably confirm or put to rest the idea that Father Thigpen is actually Miles Tate if we can get hold of a photo of Miles Tate. Or, failing that, find someone who knew him back in Boston – someone under the age of ninety-five with an unclouded memory – and show him or her the photo we have of Father Thigpen. Kate, your friend's friend who knew the Newbury Street art scene in 1990 – what about her?"

Once again, Kate reached for her phone as her cat looked on unconcernedly.

Within 15 minutes, Kate had the name and email address of one Noreen Mellinger, who was assistant curator at an art gallery just up the street from the Khachaturian establishment 31 years earlier. Kate sent her our photo of Father Thigpen and asked if this man resembled Miles Tate as she remembered him. Within seconds, Ms. Mellinger replied: "Could be him. Not sure. The hair is all wrong – I think Miles shaved his head – but the ironical smile looks right."

A priest with an ironical smile? Kate, Timmy, and I all agreed that this particular priest might have had his reasons.

CHAPTER 22

THE PLAN WAS TO DRIVE back to Albany for the night and pick up our funeral suits. Timmy was the possessor of an extensive wardrobe befitting the minion to a princeling of the New York State Legislature. I had one dark suit that I'd had made in Bangkok some years earlier at a fraction of what the cost in Albany would have been. As the elegant garment had hung in the closet over the years and been taken out and worn only infrequently, something had nibbled at one of the pants cuffs. Covid had prevented a return trip to Thailand for a replacement, but I had done what fixing up I could on the damaged garment with a small scissors, a glue stick, and a black Sharpie.

We stayed in Lenox long enough to join Kate for Chinese takeout we'd picked up at a place on the Pittsfield-Lenox Road (Timmy paid). She was feeling despondent again. Her daughter Samantha had phoned from Fiji asking for another gift or just loan. She and her boyfriend Bill were trying to earn money tutoring English-language students, but they were not making ends meet.

Kate had had to decline Sam's request, saying she was sorry but she did not have any extra cash. Timmy and I overheard her suggest that the two young people return to Lenox and help her out at the B&B, and they could live there until they found work at home. She pointed out that international

117

travel was possible again for people who had been vaccinated. Fiji had been slow at first, but then caught up, and nearly everybody on the island was well immunized, including Samantha and Bill.

That's when Kate was informed that the cash the Peace Corps in Thailand had provided the two young volunteers to make their own travel arrangements for returning to the U.S. had gotten them as far as Fiji, and they had spent most of the rest of the money on their beachfront cottage rental.

Next came a tense exchange. Nothing was resolved, and there were tears on both ends. I wondered if Timmy might bring out his MasterCard a second time. But he stayed out of it, except to sympathize and then to pay for the steamed snow peas and the General Tso's chicken.

Over the Chinese dinner served up in Kate's kitchen, Timmy carefully brought up the subject again. He asked if there was a way he could be helpful, quickly adding that he couldn't think of what that might be. The subtext being, probably not the MasterCard this time.

"It's just so exasperating," Kate said. "I was so happy and proud when Sam joined the Peace Corps. The Peace Corps was the best thing I ever did, and I knew deep down it would be the same for Sam. I don't know what I ever did for India – that whole poultry development project was a borderline fiasco – but I know what the experience did for me, and I wished it would be the same for Sam. I mean, knowing – really *knowing* – how the other half of the human race lives. And connecting with at least a few people in just such a lovely personal way. But she was only in Thailand for two months before Covid hit, and that, unfortunately, was that."

"Well," Timmy said, "she met Bill there. That seems to be a good thing, no?"

Another head wobble. "I guess so. Of course, I've never met him. But they do seem to be a match. They seem to bring out the best in each other – kindness, generosity, adaptability. But maybe the worst, too. Such as lah-de-dah, no need to be overly concerned with where the next meal is coming from, or the next roof over anybody's head. It's the one way I think I might have failed preparing Sam for the real world. Growing up, she studied and did sports and had fun. Even after her dad died and money was tight, I never suggested she help out and work a few hours at McDonald's or whatever. Then at Smith, she had her scholarship. And in Thailand she had her Peace Corps living allowance. Now it's just, 'Oh, gosh darn, we're flat out of rupees. How the heck did *that* happen? I guess I'd better call Mom!'"

Timmy and I sat listening to Kate, both of us feeling helpless. What could we say? Only Arthur appeared unmoved.

"Sometimes," Kate said, her serving of Mandarin chicken only half eaten, "I feel as if I indulged Samantha the same way Aunt Mary indulged Bucky. Except, Bucky revered his mother – and I am sure deeply reveres her memory – and Sam pretty much takes me for granted. I know she loves me in her way. But sometimes it seems as if I'm not a mother so much as a kind of mother figure. And, as you are now well aware, a kind of mother-slash-ATM."

This was treacherous territory we were headed into, so care was called for.

Timmy said, "Well, your daughter turned out to be a kind and caring and helpful human being. Bucky Costello turned out to be a thief. A volatile creep of a guy. A total jerk. So by comparing yourself to your mostly harmless but in some ways deeply problematical aunt, you're being terribly unfair to yourself, Kate."

"Do you know that Bucky had a basket of fruit delivered to Aunt Mary on most major holidays? He rarely showed up in person, but he knew that his mom loved strawberries, so he always asked that extra strawberries be included in the delivery."

"Maybe," Timmy said, "he didn't visit his mother in person because at some level – what with the Gardner art treasures hidden in your Aunt Mary's living room – he thought of his own mother as a kind of Bonnie Parker. And he was the Clyde Barrow who had made her that way."

Kate winced. "One thing I'm sure of. If it ever comes out that Bucky was one of the Gardner thieves – and if we have our way, that is quite soon going to happen – Bucky will definitely not want it known that his mother was involved in any way in the heist and the thirty-year aftermath. He would do *anything* to keep Aunt Mary's reputation unsullied."

Whenever I had thought about tracking Bucky Costello down, I had wondered what I could possibly say to him to make him confess to what he had done, and to make him reveal what he knew about where the Gardner art might be at the present time. And now, thanks to Kate, I knew what approach to take.

CHAPTER 23

IT WAS THURSDAY NIGHT, and Bucky was still in Boston. Significantly – or so it seemed to me – he was again somewhere in the vicinity of Fenway Park. Back at home in Albany, I phoned the Red Sox corporate office – which had the same address on New Jersey Avenue as the stadium – and asked how I might reach Walter Costello. But it was after nine at night, and the guy who answered the phone had no information about this particular Sox employee. He suggested I call back in the morning. I planned to do more than just phone.

Before I crawled into bed with Timothy before 11 and turned on the upstairs TV to see what Trevor Noah was making of the day's events, I checked Bucky's location once again. He was still at or near Fenway Park. I looked up the Sox game that night with the Yanks. It was still going on in the top of the ninth with the Yankees leading 4 to 3. So maybe Bucky was in the stands? Possibly back at work?

Another game was scheduled for Friday night, and that confirmed my idea to head for Boston in the morning and see if I could somehow track Bucky down at or near the ballpark. Kate had sent me a copy of the most recent photo she had of Bucky. It was taken at the funeral of her Uncle Lewis, Bucky's dad, eleven years earlier. Bucky was in green pants and a brown sport coat with a red tie that had a picture of Ted Williams on it. Kate's cousin was a broad-jawed man of medium stature with a red nose and tired gray eyes.

At 11:17, *bleep bleep*, a text appeared. It was from Laurel Peaseley at Strathmore.

> Hi. Just circling back to find out if Strathmore is still on your radar. You are certainly on ours, Donald! Please know that the company's Asuncion office was just named the premier investigative agency in Paraguay for the third year in a row! Our Albany office is just a ten-minute walk from your adorable little house on Crow Street, so you wouldn't necessarily have to relocate! And your cutie-pie main squeeze Timothy Callahan could continue his employment in the office of Assemblyman Myron Lipschitz, who I'm sure is familiar with Strathmore's occasional jobs on behalf of the Democratic Party of New York! Anyway, just checking in. Have a wonderful Thursday night, and looking forward to hearing back from you on the morrow!

I read this aloud to Timmy. He said, "Oh boy."

"Do I really want to work for an outfit that talks like that?"

We had a window open to the abnormally warm June night air – global warming at its sweetest – and the bare leg he'd draped over mine he now withdrew. "What do you think she means when she says Strathmore has done jobs for the state Democratic Party? Into whom or what might those investigations have been?"

"And how do they know our house is quote-unquote adorable?"

"And what kind of investigative agency uses language like that, anyway?"

"And how and why do they know or care that you work for Myron?"

He muted the TV in Trevor Noah's mid-sentence. "I guess it makes sense that they'd vet you pretty thoroughly before offering you a job. And spouses would have to be part of that vetting."

"They know we're married to each other. I put that on my application. I wonder if they also know that when we first met way back when it was on a hot summer night under a bush in Washington Park. As I clearly recall, a few people were nearby watching us, with their hands on their dicks. I wonder if one of them was reporting back to the Strathmore office."

"Or more likely, back then, the Albany Police Department."

"And how," I asked indignantly, "does Strathmore know that you are a cutie-pie? I don't think I mentioned that on the forms I filled out."

A downcast look. "You didn't?"

"The Strathmore folks seem to be quite the overly informed buttinskies. Do they know your Blue Cross-Blue Shield account number? Your hat size? About the Ireland-shaped birthmark on your left butt cheek?"

"Of course," Timmy mused, "if you were the HR person at Strathmore, you'd make it your business to know as much as you possibly could about anybody you were considering hiring for such sensitive work. You'd have to be assured that the potential hire had no sizeable skeletons in his or her closet."

"Do I have any skeletons that are still *in my closet*? Hey, that's a good one."

"You do have a tendency to wear your skeletons on your sleeve."

"Or on my chest, like the major general in Gilbert and Sullivan."

"Strathmore has no doubt asked the Albany cops what their opinion is of you. The cops and the business and political establishments. There are those views they'll have to consider."

"Skeletons would be found, yes, but closets, no," I reminded the cutie-pie. "Anyhow, Strathmore is famously results-oriented in its approach to detective work. And they have undoubtedly found that that's always been the case with me, also."

"I'm glad," Timmy said, giving me some leg again, "that we wouldn't necessarily have to move to Paraguay. Are there still Nazis hiding out down there?"

"The thing that really gets me," I said, "is that the text said they hoped to hear from me *on the morrow*. I mean, would you want to work for an organization who had somebody on their payroll who talked like that? I mean, would you?"

"No."

"Then it's settled."

"It is? Fine with me."

After a moment of thought, and a bit of memory jogging concerning my finances, I said, "Of course that wordage is such a trivial thing."

Timmy laughed. "Not to me it isn't," and then I had to laugh, too.

Just before we turned the lights out a little after midnight, I checked Bucky's location again. He was still somewhere in the vicinity of Fenway Park. I checked the ball game and it had ended just after 11, and the Sox had come back and beat the Yankees 5 to 4. So what was Bucky doing at or near Fenway more than an hour later? Could he somehow sleep overnight at the ballpark? Did he have another girlfriend in the vicinity he could spend the night with and not have to drive back to Belmont and face Janice's wrath over the theft of her 400 dollars?

It was as puzzling as ever, and it only made me more eager than ever to head to Lenox in the morning and then on to the city where Bucky was currently maneuvering, as was, apparently, the elusive Father Mike Thigpen.

CHAPTER 24

NOBODY AT THE BALL PARK knew where Bucky was. He had the week off from work – "bereavement leave," a woman in an office told me – and they thought he would be back the following week, but nobody was quite sure.

I had driven Timmy back to Lenox early Friday morning in my Camry, more commodious than his little Honda, and dropped off the cutie-pie and our Saturday funeral-wear at Kate's house. She was still feeling anxious about (a) the severe financial pressure she was under and (b) the disputatious and emotionally draining conversation she had had with her daughter in Fiji. Timmy planned to spend the day with his old pal and try to cheer her up as much as might be possible.

Kate told me Father Thigpen had not called her back about the untimely death of his sister Martha. We doubted he would, the guy not being stupid. So I still lacked the priest's phone number. Only Bucky had that – *if* Thigpen was actually Miles Tate. If he wasn't, then where was I?

I did pick up one useful lead as to Bucky's whereabouts. A maintenance man at Fenway who knew Bucky a little said he thought he'd seen Costello the night before at a tavern up the street from the stadium called Jim-bo's. This guy said he thought Bucky went there often and I should look in later.

I found Jim-bo's, where even before noon a bunch of what

looked like the bar's well-worn regulars had established themselves on stools below the TV sets tuned to ESPN. Except for the electronics, the place looked as if it had not changed since 1936. The blown-up black-and-white photos on the walls were of Sox greats from "Smoky Joe" Wood in 1908 to Carl Yastrzemski, 1961 to '83, to the present-day David Ortiz. And taking up much of a side wall was a shrine dedicated to the Splendid Splinter, Ted Williams, with photos, trophies, balls, bats – *bats!* – and a uniform bearing the number 9, that number having been retired in 1984. I looked around for a freezer that might have contained Williams' frozen remains, but none was visible to my untrained eye.

I found an empty stool and told the bartender, who looked as if he could have served Dom DiMaggio or even Smoky Joe, I was looking for my old high school baseball teammate Bucky Costello, and had he seen Bucky lately?

"Yeah, Bucky came in yesterday around when I was leaving at four. I don't see him in here now, but maybe later." He had the Boston accent down pat, pronouncing *four* something like *faw,* and *later* like *late-eh.* I figured he nailed me as some kind of *farang*, but he wasn't unfriendly about it.

"Yeah, I'd love to run into him," I said. "It happens we're both trying to locate somebody, and I need to talk to the Buckster about that."

"Like a criminal is it you're looking for?"

"Not exactly, but maybe sort of. Why do you ask that?"

"I saw yesterday Bucky was talking to some police officers. We get cops in here from the precinct. There's a couple over there at a table by Johnny Pesky right now. So maybe Bucky was looking for information from law enforcement."

I noted that Johnny Pesky was not a customer but a photo of a player in a Sox uniform. "Well, I wouldn't approach those officers, since I don't know them. But Bucky has cop friends? I'm glad to hear that."

"Not that he's palsy-walsy. In fact, I never saw him fraternizing with the law before. But I guess he did it yesterday because he was trying to locate whoever it is you're looking for. Who is it? Probably nobody I'd know."

"I don't suppose so."

"But I've been bartending in this shit shack for thirty-two years, so you never know."

The barkeep served a few other customers, and then I called him back over. "Do you get any clergy coming in here? I suppose, why not?"

"Sure, we do. Is that who you're looking for? A pastor?"

"He might be. That's part of something I'm trying to figure out. Though Bucky might not know that part. I'm not sure."

Now the guy was looking confused. He had thinning white hair, a sharp beak, and a small scab on his bony chin where it looked as if he might have nicked himself shaving. The place was getting busier, and at the tables some people were ordering food from waitresses, one young, another who might have served Johnny Pesky a burger, medium-well. Not wanting to be a free-loader, I asked for a Sprite. I saw the bartender size me up as AA, and that would be okay as long as I tipped. Which I did, planning to return later in the day.

So, Bucky the ex-criminal was hanging out with cops? What was *that* about?

I checked my phone for Bucky's current location. To my amazement, he was on the Mass Pike, I-90, just outside Boston, headed west. Toward the Berkshires, but was he going that far? If he was, that was good. Wasn't it?

My impulse was to hop into the Camry and follow Bucky. But first I wanted to talk to the cops he was hanging out with late yesterday afternoon and learn, if I could, what Bucky was trying to learn from them – which I now had my suspicions about – and how did he make out?

Meanwhile, I knew where I wanted to spend the next few hours.

CHAPTER 25

JUST A TEN-MINUTE DRIVE from the ballpark, the Isabella Stewart Gardner Museum had been modeled after a fifteenth century Venetian Palazzo that Mrs. Gardner and her wealthy husband liked to stay in on their visits to Italy. On one trip to Venice, Mrs. Gardner purchased many of the columns, reliefs, balustrades, and other architectural features for the building she put up to house her extensive art collection. When it opened in 1902, the museum was one of the most illustrious additions to a neighborhood that had until only recently been an uninhabited swamp.

I was mainly interested in taking a look at the infamous side door the hapless guards had opened one late night in March 1990, to let the two fake cops in, and to view the empty frames the museum had hung up to remind visitors of what had been lost. I did see all of those and was especially moved by the gaping hole where Rembrandt's large *Storm Over the Sea of Galilee* had been sliced out and rolled up, never to be seen again by art lovers who still came to the Gardner by the hundreds of thousands.

I wandered around the place – only a little crowded even on a Friday – gazing happily at the Tintorettos and Sargents and Manets, and also enjoying the museum's courtyard with its unlikely hodgepodge of architectural details, and a light that, according to a museum brochure, felt as if it had been reflected off water, as in Venice.

The item that made the biggest impression on me was the Rembrandt self-portrait, an early acquisition by Mrs. Gardner, and painted when the artist was just 23. In it, Rembrandt didn't look the way he often later appeared, wry, or sly, or cocky, or borderline-distraught – *Am I going to end up penniless?* (he did) – but with a youthful funny mixture of earnestness and bemusement: *This is all so great, but what next???*

Which were my thoughts exactly. *What next?* Part of me wanted to locate the museum's P-A system and announce: *Attention! Attention! You all are probably aware that seventeen wonderful items are missing from this grand institution since a daring robbery that took place on St. Patrick's Day night in 1990. But rest assured that I am on the trail of the missing great art works, and they will soon be returned! So please come back for another visit when that happens! Thank you, and have a nice rest of your day!*

If I had done that, I would have been taken for some kind of madman and expelled from the premises, at least. But among the several thoughts that held me back from making such a proclamation was a sense of unreality. Could *I* actually be the instrument of the missing art treasures' safe return? After all the years of investigations involving hundreds – maybe thousands – of federal, state, and city law officers, could an aging PI from Albany wander into these proceedings and actually accomplish what none of the skilled and dedicated professionals could do?

That just seemed nuts. I was briefly light-headed, and I began to feel as if I were a kind of delusional Donald Trump: *Only I can do it.*

And yet. Kate Webster's story, and her Aunt Mary's confession, and Fess Tetlow's offhand confirmation of what he told me he and Bucky had pulled off almost as a lark at the behest of a crooked Newberry Street art dealer – it all seemed as plausible as any other explanation for the great heist.

So, no. I regained my wits and believed once again that

I hadn't gone around the bend, and if I just tried harder, and I had a run of luck, I would recover the Rembrandts and the Vermeer and all the other lost paintings and artifacts, and soon the empty frames would again hold their thrilling balm for the human mind and eyes into a long and gratifying future.

Outside the museum, I checked my phone to see where Bucky was. He was approaching Lenox.

CHAPTER 26

BACK AT JIM-BO'S, an after-work crowd was gathering. The bartender I'd talked to earlier – I now learned his name was Marty – had already cashed out and was about to head out the door. He remembered me and pointed at two guys at a table who he said were BPD plain clothes and were "good guys, but not *too* good."

"My kind of cops," I said.

I carried a Sam Adams over and told the two officers that Marty spoke well of them as people who might help me out locating somebody.

"Who would that be?"

He was the older of the two, my age, with close-cropped hair on a big head and squinty blue eyes. The younger guy, also in khakis and a dark sport coat, was muscular and baby-faced.

"Bucky Costello, who works for the Sox. We played high school ball together. Marty told me you know the Buckster and he was in here yesterday. I'm sorry I missed the ornery dickwad."

Sometimes my attempting to use *het-speak* – as Timmy liked to call it – as an ice-breaker didn't work. But it seemed to this time.

"Yeah, Bucky Costello," the younger cop said. "He was in here yesterday." He had a high-pitched voice with the same accent as Marty.

"Your old teammate was looking for somebody too," the older cop offered. "Maybe he was looking for you." He watched me to see how I reacted to that.

"I doubt that. There's no reason he would. I don't think he even knows I'm in Boston. I live in East Liverpool, Ohio."

"Anyway, he didn't have a name. Just a phone number."

Bingo.

"What do you mean by that? Just a number."

"Your pal had a cell phone number, and he was looking to find out who it belonged to."

"That's weird."

"Maybe you don't know... What's your name?"

"Donald."

"I'm Paul and this is William. When was the last time you saw your old schoolmate, Donald?"

"Whoa. It's been a while."

"Was he a law-abiding citizen back in whenever it was?"

"As far as I know."

"Then it looks like you don't know that that's not exactly the man Mr. Costello is at the present time."

William snickered. "Costello had four hundred dollars' worth of box seats for a Sox-Astros double-header next month. He was giving them away to any police officer who would find out and tell him who a phone number belonged to. Box seats! I mean, fuck."

Paul concurred. "That's a serious infraction, using official methods to obtain private information for personal reasons."

"Jeez," I said.

"So we told your buddy we would not be able to help him out," Paul said.

"I wonder why Bucky would want to do that. How strange."

William laughed. "He said he was just helping out the department. He was recovering stolen goods. It sounded to me like B-S."

"What kind of stolen goods? Like TVs or cases of Johnny Walker? What are we talking about here? This is not the Bucky I knew back in Lenox."

"Not Ohio?"

"Doreen and I live out there now, but Bucky and I grew up in Lenox. It's out in the Berkshires."

Paul said, "It was some valuable paintings. Costello went on about some high-priced art some dude had swiped from him, and he was going to do us all a great favor by recovering it."

I said, "Maybe it's the Gardner Museum heist paintings. The Mona Lisa, or whatever it was. That would be pretty amazing."

They both nodded and chuckled. "It sure would be," Paul said.

William added, "And your pal would get the reward. How much is it now? Twenty million?"

"Not that much," his colleague corrected him. "It was five, then ten, then back down to five. I think it's back up to ten."

"That was a big thing in Boston," I said. "We even heard about it in Ohio. And nobody knows who did it, right?"

"Wiseguys, probably," Paul said. "And then the paintings got lost somewhere before whoever did it could unload them."

"I wonder how the Buckster ever got involved with recovering stolen art. As far as I know, he just works for the Red Sox. Maybe it's a hobby of his."

They were drinking drafts out of mugs, and William took a big swig. "Whatever the deal is, your friend is pretty determined to track this person down. I don't know how he's gonna make out, really. I hate to say this, Donald, but Costello didn't strike me as somebody playing with a full deck."

"Is that why you didn't take him up on his offer? He struck you as too unreliable a personality to get mixed up with? Or too dishonest? Or both?"

They both laughed. "Something like that," Paul said, and they looked at each other.

"So," I said, "it sounds as if Bucky must have left the bar

last night disappointed."

They chuckled again. Paul: "We suggested he might try a couple of fellow officers we know and pointed them out. We headed home early, but Bucky was at the bar and he thanked us on our way out. He said our colleagues on the force had liked the idea of the Sox-Astros tickets, and they were going to see what they could do, and they'd be back in here around eleven o'clock last night. I guess maybe that all worked out, because Mr. Costello doesn't seem to have been in here all day today."

CHAPTER 27

"NOW I'M WONDERING," I told Timmy and Kate, "if I shouldn't have stayed in Boston and tracked down the cops who apparently told Bucky what he needed to know. That is, who Miles Tate's phone number actually belongs to."

Timmy gave me the head wobble. "Could you have?"

"I had nothing to offer those guys in exchange. No four hundred dollars' worth of box seats. They didn't know me at all, and I wouldn't have come recommended by fellow cops, the way Bucky had. Also, my standard mid-Atlantic American speech patterns could have been a handicap in that setting."

We were seated around Kate's kitchen table again. I'd arrived back in Lenox just after nine, delayed by the Friday night stream of traffic pouring out of Boston. She had offered me a peanut butter and jelly sandwich, but I saw that that was not going to work with the last of the Azerbaijani beer, and I had some cheese and crackers instead.

"Maybe I should have tried my luck with the rule-breaking cops, though. Now Bucky has turned off his phone, and I'm not even sure he's in Lenox. It looked like he had it on until he got off the interstate in Lee, and then nada. No signal."

"He could have run out of juice," Kate suggested. "That happens to me if I go to Boston and back and forget to recharge."

"My fear is," I said, "that the cops Bucky got his informa-

137

tion from might have told him about cell-phone tracking of the type I'm using and how he could have gotten within a quarter of a mile of his target even without an exact I-D. And then Bucky – dim as he might be – figured out that somebody could be tracking *him*, and he shut off his phone."

Arthur walked into the room, stood for a long moment, then turned and walked out again.

"What about Father Thigpen?" Timmy asked. "I take it there was no sign of him at – what was the bar called?"

"Jim-bo's. No, no clergy on the premises at all, as far as I could tell. Of course, I didn't drive around and check each Legal Seafoods restaurant."

"We could try the rectory in Pittsfield again. See if the good father – and possible art thief – is back in the Berkshires."

"It's getting late to call," Kate said, and refilled her red wine glass. Was she overdoing it? She wasn't tipsy.

"Anyway," Timmy said, "if those Pittsfield priests are complicit in whatever Thigpen is up to, they sure as heck aren't going to tell you where he is or anything else about him. You'd have to come up with a pretty good story in order to pry any information out of them."

I got annoyed with Father Moyer all over again. "How about an indictment? That might loosen their tongues. Or at least a subpoena?"

"We have a description of Bucky's car," Timmy reminded me. "The red Hyundai with the Red Sox stickers on it. If he's in Lenox, we could just drive around and maybe get lucky and spot him, no?"

"You guys could try it," Kate said. "I have to stay at the house and greet my only two guests for the weekend, Phyllis and Leon Grisham. They called to say they'd be late, and they're in town having dinner. But you two could look around. That car should stand out around here, that's for sure. In Lenox, in order to put stickers on your car anywhere except on the rear bumper you'd probably have to get a zoning variance."

I agreed that we had nothing to lose by having a look around Lenox and environs. Mary Costello's funeral was not until ten o'clock the next morning. There was still the off-chance that Bucky would show up at his mother's funeral after having told the funeral director he would not be able to attend. But we could not count on that, so it made sense for us to try to locate him by way of any crude means we could come up with.

What *was* Bucky doing back in the area? And was Miles Tate, aka Father Mike Thigpen, also back in the Berkshires and was about to get pounced on by a man with a baseball bat who wanted his valuable paintings back?

I was also eager for something to eat. The only food in Kate's fridge besides a jar of jelly was meant for her paying guests' breakfasts, and Timmy and I were freeloaders. I saw on my phone there was a Burger King on the Pittsfield-Lenox Road, so we headed in that direction. The GPS took us out to the main highway past Mary Costello's house on Walker Street, and we noted that the place was dark and no car was parked in the driveway.

On the way up the Pittsfield-Lenox road we noticed some of the new hotels that, along with a proliferation of B&Bs, had so depleted Kate's business. We swung through the parking lots of a couple of these places on the lookout for Bucky's red Hyundai, even though Bucky had apparently spent the 400 dollars he'd swiped from Janice on the Sox box-seat tickets and probably couldn't afford the Brandywine-Sussex Guest Suites At Lenox – which, despite its pompous moniker and its recent construction, resembled a state mental hospital in 1947.

Along a commercial strip where the Burger King welcomed us, there were some cheaper, far less grand, old-style motels – the kind that used to have a sign out front advertising *Color TV* – but we didn't spot Bucky's car at any of those, either.

We each gobbled down a Whopper with cheese in the Burger King parking lot (Timmy paid) and watched the voluminous Friday night traffic pass by, hoping to lay eyes on the Hyundai, but with no luck.

We soon made our way back to the part of town that had barely changed in a hundred and fifty years – a directional sign out on the highway called it *Historic Lenox* – and cruised around side streets looking for Bucky's car outside any of the pretty old houses. We didn't find it.

Back at Kate's place on serene Undermountain Road, a mile or two from the town center, we gave her the disappointing news that we had not been lucky enough to stumble upon her renegade cousin.

We were about to launch into a discussion on what we might do next when Kate's weekend paying guests arrived, the Grishams from New York. She greeted them warmly – they had stayed with her before – and they told her about the nice dinner they had just enjoyed in town at a sushi place on Housatonic Street.

Phyllis Grisham also informed us that something had been going on around the corner on Church Street that involved a number of police cars with their lights flashing. She and her husband did not know what the commotion was about, and Kate, Timmy, and I did not make anything much of this report at the time.

CHAPTER 28

THERE HAD BEEN A FEW showers overnight, but now the sun was breaking through as we stood on the steps of St. Agnes Church on Main Street on the edge of the downtown Lenox business district. We arrived at 9:30, in plenty of time for the 10 o'clock funeral Mass conducted by Father Sondergaard.

Timmy was characteristically bespoke in his State Assembly get-up, I was in my popular-with-the-mice Bangkok dark suit, and Kate was lovely in a Prussian blue silk dress. She had planted herself on the church's top step to greet mourners and receive their condolences, and Timmy and I stood nearby, no doubt leading many of the locals to wonder, *Who are those two?*

Those who came earliest were the St. Agnes Mass regulars, Kate told us, mostly retirees of both sexes who might or might not have been friends of the deceased. Many were nicely turned out, although a few were dressed as if they had just popped in as an afterthought during a run out to pick up some bathtub stain remover. Some wore masks, most not. Timmy and I had ours on but with our nostrils exposed, probably irking both sides in the mask tribal wars.

Soon to arrive after the early birds were Mary Costello's garden club and church group pals. Mostly women in their seventies and eighties, they told Kate one by one, or sometimes in twos, that they were sorry for her loss. Kate thanked them all and warmly embraced several, including two who declared that their friend Mary was now "in a better place."

One of Mrs. Costello's friends, Evelyn Trimble, who was known for being "outspoken," overheard the "better place" remark, and said to Kate, "A better place than Lenox? I don't think so."

Aunt Mary's better place at the moment was a tasteful but decidedly mid-range casket that had been hauled up the steps by pallbearers the church had called upon from among its congregation. The dignified container now rested in the foyer of the nicely proportioned stone structure. Kate had continued to hold out at least a smidgen of hope that Bucky would surprise us all and join the bearers of his beloved mother's remains. But he was not among the six middle-aged men who had huffed and puffed to get the casket up the steps, after which they moved to the rear of the sanctuary.

Hank Thurmer arrived scowling, nodded to us – those two Albany types – and said to Kate within our earshot, "I suppose you heard what happened last night."

"Happened where? What are you referring to, Hank?"

"Lenox's latest crime wave. You don't know about it?"

"I don't think so."

"Sean Cunard was attacked in his art gallery. Some expensive art was stolen."

"Oh no!"

"Cunard is in BMC with serious injuries. Who are they going to come after next? None of us are safe anymore. It's ridiculous, just ridiculous!"

I could all but hear the wheels turning in Kate's head. "That's awful. What was the art that was stolen? Does anybody know?"

"Two of Marcel's ballerinas. A couple of the smaller ones. People pay good money for those things, though I've never understood why."

"Did they catch who did it?"

"Not as far as I've heard. But I have acquaintances in the department, and I'll find out."

"Violent crime is so rare in Lenox. It's really kind of shocking."

Thurmer snorted. "You're shocked? I guess you haven't been paying attention for the last fifty years. Anyway, Kate, I am sorry for your loss."

As Thurmer moved on inside the church, Kate turned to Timmy and me. "Did you hear that?"

I said we did.

"I'm trying to process it," Timmy murmured.

Kate said, "Me, too."

More people entered the church, and Kate said, "Who do you think those guys were?"

She was referring to two stocky men in dark suits, blue ties and well shined black shoes who had eased past us and strode inside. They appeared to be in their forties, not geezer-ish like nearly everybody else, and what did that mean?

Kate said, "They looked like they could be – what? FBI?"

"I wouldn't think so" Timmy said. "How would the feds know anything about anything at this point?"

Three of Kate's old colleagues from the *Eagle* arrived and told her how sorry they were about her aunt and said let's get together soon. She told them, you bet.

Just before ten, with only a few stragglers still on the front steps, a beautifully dressed man with a gray pompadour arrived and greeted Kate through a black mask. After confirming who she was, he said he was so sorry about her aunt, and he introduced himself as Terry McGonigal, the funeral director.

"Oh," Kate said, "you didn't need to come down here yourself, Mr. McGonigal. But I do appreciate it." I wondered if he was sizing her up as a potential deadbeat, her credit card having been declined earlier.

"I felt as if I needed to talk to you personally," McGonigal said. "I wasn't sure if your cousin Walter had contacted you or not."

"Bucky. The family calls him Bucky. No, we have not been in touch. In fact, I've been trying for days to reach him."

"But you knew he would not be attending the funeral today, is that not correct?"

"One of your staff informed me of that on Tuesday. Yes, I knew."

"He told Jack Reilly, one of our grief counsellors, that he was too distraught, and he was afraid he would just be a distraction, and that you had a lot on your mind, and he didn't want to cause you any more grief than you were already feeling."

I could see that Kate was trying hard not to laugh. "Uh-huh."

"Jack said your cousin's grief was very profound. And this morning I saw that for myself."

A bell sounded, indicating it was time to go inside.

"You saw Bucky? You spoke with him?" First her eyes were wide and then they narrowed.

"I thought he was going to tell you. He said he would. Walter was in Pittsfield and came by the mortuary a few hours ago. He explained again that he was too emotionally fragile to attend the funeral. And that he preferred to say goodbye to his mother privately."

Kate said, "Jesus."

"He spent ten minutes alone with her. He was weeping when he arrived and he was weeping when he left. I almost called you to alert you as to the state your cousin was in. But then I thought, no, that's not my place. I hope I was right about that."

Kate assured McGonigal he had probably done the right thing according to the protocols of his profession.

After he left us to go inside, Kate looked at Timmy and me. "What the fuck?"

Then we walked inside, too.

CHAPTER 29

WE SAT IN THE "FAMILY" section in the front pews. There weren't many of us. Just Kate, Timmy and me, a couple of distant Winkleman cousins from Tyringham, and a Costello niece who had driven over from Amherst. Kate's father, Lewis Costello's brother Edward, had died too young, in his sixties, of leukemia. Her mother Betty had been lost several years later to liver cancer. Other Costellos were scattered across North America, Kate had told us. They had been notified of Mary Costello's passing by Cousin Annabella, in Akron, the family member who kept track of these things and made sure people were informed.

Several relatives had had bouquets of cut flowers ordered online and sent to the church. Kate didn't know if these were from people who were just poorly informed or if something passive-aggressive was going on. Either way, these floral tributes were set off to the side away from Aunt Mary's boxed remains.

As the funeral Mass proceeded with a good deal of Catholic standing up, sitting down, and kneeling, Kate took every opportunity to glance around and see who had shown up for the sad occasion. There was no Bucky, of course, and no Father Thigpen – not that any of us expected him to get anywhere near Lenox, the site of an art theft that he may have been the perpetrator of.

But *had* he been? Now we had another extremely interesting person of interest.

The two men Kate had tagged as FBI agents were seated together in a pew near the rear. I doubted her ID of the two was correct. It was a crude stereotype she had fallen back on. But then, who were they? Debt collectors sent by Visa?

The personable but now solemn Father Sondergaard conducted the Mass with what felt like accustomed purpose and efficiency. When it came time for the eulogy, we all paid close attention. He went on for several minutes about Mary Costello's Christian faith and the good works that faith had inspired. He referred to the Garden Club, her membership in the St. Agnes Sodality, and her "dedication to preserving the Earth's natural resources." The priest mentioned that Mrs. Costello was also a competent amateur painter.

Additionally, Father Sondergaard told the story of how Mrs. Costello had lost a tooth crown on the trail up to hilltop Kennedy Park one time, how a number of St. Agnes parishioners had gotten down on their hands and knees to help her find it, and how Albany TV had reported on the event. This produced appreciative chuckles throughout the sanctuary.

The priest mentioned almost in passing that Mary Costello had been "a loving mother," without going into any specifics, or saying whom she had been a loving mother to.

Kate muttered, "Loving mother. This guy doesn't know the half of it."

I whispered back, "I doubt there's anything in Catholic doctrine requiring a priest giving a eulogy to outline a family member's criminal record. I know that Presbyterians don't have to do it."

Timmy did not look at us, but we could hear him. "*Shhh.*"

Soon it was time for Holy Communion, and a number of congregants came forward to receive the blessing. Our little group stayed put, as did most of the gathering, including the two suits in the back, who, every time I looked their way, one of them looked back at me poker-faced.

Soon, more bells were rung and Aunt Mary's casket was

rolled back up the aisle by the pallbearers. We all turned and watched as it disappeared out the main doors of the sanctuary. Since there would be no additional ceremony at the gravesite in Lee – in accordance with Bucky's wishes – this was to be the last any of us would see of Mary Costello.

An usher accompanied us up the aisle, and we stood in the foyer as many of the mourners again expressed their condolences and well wishes to Kate. A few of the dottier old ladies inquired about Bucky, and Kate told them that he was "in pretty bad shape but holding his own."

There were only a few stragglers left at 11:20 when we noticed that the two unidentified men in suits, who had been loitering on the edge of the St. Agnes lawn, were making their way toward us.

One of them approached Kate and said, "Mrs. Webster?"

"Yes. Kate. I'm Mrs. Costello's niece."

"Special Agent Glenn Trout, Federal Bureau of Investigation. This is Special Agent Dean G. Brisbane. May we have a word with you?"

I could see between 20 and 30 expressions flash across Kate's face in a matter of a few seconds. "Oh, sure."

She introduced Timmy and me to the two men, and we all nodded but, following the pandemic protocols, didn't shake hands.

"FBI. Wow. What brings you two to my aunt's funeral? I'm surprised. Did you know her?"

"No," Trout said, "we were not acquainted with your aunt. However, we have some information about her that we would like to discuss with you."

"Information about Aunt Mary that the FBI would be interested in? Well, there's a shocker."

Kate chuckled, but the two feds just stared.

"Would it be all right if Timothy and Donald were with me for our discussion? I've been pretty much a mess emotionally throughout the ordeal of losing my favorite aunt, and they've been so wonderful in their constant support."

They hesitated, but then Trout nodded.

"Timothy is my old pal from when we were in the Peace Corps together many years ago," Kate said, eliciting another blank stare. Was this some kind of interrogation technique? Let the interviewee blather on until a confession of some type tumbles out?

"We'll take up as little of your time as possible," Trout said. "Then we must get back on the pike and return to Boston. We are affiliated with the Bureau's Boston Field Office."

"This is very mysterious," Kate said. "Goodness. Why don't we sit over there?" She indicated two benches across the street in a small park shaded by two towering oak trees.

Was this the moment to make a break for it? Maybe hijack a visiting New Yorker's Saab and flee north on Main Street, the two feds hurling hot lead as we sped away? It didn't seem practical.

CHAPTER 30

ONCE WE WERE ALL SEATED on the park benches, Agent Trout announced, "Our office has had a report that your Aunt Mary Costello possessed information about a crime committed in the city of Boston in the year 1990. Are you aware of this?"

"Aware of this report? No, this is the first time I am hearing about it."

"A citizen informant visited our office on Tuesday of this week – that would be four days ago – and this informant claimed prior to your aunt's passing to have received information directly from Mary Costello concerning the theft of highly valuable art objects from the Isabella Stewart Gardner Museum in Boston on March 18, 1990. Are you familiar with that event?"

"Of course. It was a famous crime at the time. The Gardner Rembrandt heist." She was doing a fantastic job of keeping a straight face, although a sandaled foot was jiggling a bit.

I said, "I don't think that case has ever been solved, has it?" They looked over at me stolidly, and I hoped my remark was not taken as an implied criticism of the FBI. Even though that's what it was.

Agent Brisbane spoke up now. "The case is still open. It's something the Bureau takes extremely seriously, recovering all those famous paintings. We follow up every lead, no matter how whacko it sounds. In Boston, that heist was a big deal." I could hear him thinking big *fucking* deal, but he didn't say it.

"But how in the world," Kate asked with a small smile, "would my Aunt Mary know anything about the Gardner Museum robbery? She being here in Lenox basically all of her life."

I was trying to remember what the law was on lying to the FBI. Was it a crime only if you were under investigation? Or you were a public official? Or could making stuff up in an interview like this get you indicted?

Agent Trout peered over at Kate gravely. Cars cruised past us on Main Street, all of them slowing to 20 mph as they passed the electronic sign flashing the words *SLOW DOWN*.

Trout said, "Shortly before she passed, your aunt spoke to a man of the cloth. Were you aware of that?"

"Do you mean a clergyman?"

"Correct."

"Aunt Mary was religious. So she would have done that."

Agent Brisbane had his device out now and was reading something on it. "Mrs. Webster, are you acquainted with a Father Michael Thigpen?"

"I know the name."

"Have you ever met him or spoken with him?"

"No, I haven't. But I believe he was the priest from Pittsfield who heard Aunt Mary's final confession at the Mount Mercy nursing home. Anyhow, that's my understanding."

The two agents seemed to consider this, and then Agent Trout said, "Mrs. Costello had a son, Walter."

Kate's foot began to jiggle again. Were the FBI men taking note of this as some kind of "tell"?

"My cousin, Walter, yes," Kate said. "The family calls him Bucky. He wasn't at the funeral because he was so upset, he couldn't take it. Bucky and his mother were extremely close."

"Walter Costello has a criminal record. Are you aware of that?"

"I know that when he was young Bucky sometimes got in trouble. But that was a long time ago. In recent years Bucky has hewed to the straight and narrow, as far as I'm aware."

Trying to help Kate out, I said, "He works for the Sox. He's a groundskeeper at Fenway. You're a lot less inclined toward criminal activity when you've got the ghost of Ted Williams peering over your shoulder."

Ignoring that, Agent Trout said, "Father Thigpen asserted to one of our Boston agents that Mary Costello had revealed to him that her son Walter had been one of the Gardner Museum robbers. And that the stolen paintings had been hidden somewhere in Mrs. Costello's house for the past thirty years."

We all made our jaws drop.

"Father Thigpen further stated that he had advised Mrs. Costello to alert the proper authorities as to the location of the missing art. The clergyman stated additionally that your aunt told him she did not wish to notify the police because she did not wish for her son to get in trouble, was how she put it."

Kate said, "Oh my."

"She told Father Thigpen that what she would do was, she would tell her niece, Kate Webster. And that Kate Webster could find a way of returning the paintings to the museum without incriminating Walter. My question to you is: Did your aunt follow through and do that? Give you this information about your cousin and the location of the missing Gardner Museum art treasures?"

The two feds watched Kate carefully, and so did Timmy and I.

She said, "Look. Well – how can I put this?"

"What do you mean?"

Kate sighed deeply. The sigh looked genuine, and no doubt it was.

Kate explained to her interrogators that Mary Costello was a New England eccentric of a certain harmless type. That she believed, among other strange things, that the Earth's precious limited water supply was slowly being depleted by people throwing their unfinished Dr. Peppers and their undrunk ice into trash containers at places like McDonald's.

And that our precious planetary fluids were being trapped underground in non-biodegradable plastic garbage bags while the surface of the Earth gradually dried up. And that a threat to the planet equal to that of global warming was the desertification that nobody except her was doing anything about. Aunt Mary was a kind of loveable nut case, Kate said, and it didn't make sense to take anything she said about any important topic too seriously.

Neither of the two feds guffawed, or threw up his hands, or declared, "Mrs. Webster, you are quite the brazen bullshitter." They just continued to stare at her.

Nor was Kate finished. "I'm just sorry that Father Thigpen apparently swallowed my aunt's crazy Gardner Museum story hook, line, and sinker. It was obviously just one of her bizarre fantasies. I'm also sorry you officers had to take the trouble to drive all the way out here from Boston for nothing. To me, that just sucks."

The two agents soon climbed into the large black SUV they had parked illegally on the wrong side of Franklin Street and drove way.

CHAPTER 31

"NOT TO WORRY, KATE," Timmy told her. "Don and I will visit you in the Federal Penitentiary at Danbury. And they only keep the better class of criminals there. Fraud, embezzlement, what have you. Lying to the FBI. No axe murderers, I don't think."

We were back on Kate's porch. We had picked up some sandwiches at the little grocery store up the street from the church. Kate and Timmy were hitting the chardonnay again and, having depleted the supply of beer from Central Asia, I was hydrating with Lenox tap water.

"I just didn't like those guys," Kate said. "Yeah, I know, that's beside the point. The point is, *we* have to find the Gardner paintings and return them to the museum, and then collect the damn reward. And then I'll tell the FBI or anybody else who's interested everything they want to know. But not now, not yet."

I said I agreed. "The FBI has had thirty-plus years to get this right. They yanked the investigation out of the hands of the street-smart Boston cops early on, and then they botched it. So to hell with those incompetents. I'm with you, Kate."

"I'm just saying it's not a good idea to get those people mad at you," Timmy insisted. "I know, it's not the Hoover era anymore, when the FBI was often a bunch of out-of-control Brown Shirts. But they can still be vindictive if you defy them or even just embarrass them. And legally, Kate, you have no firm ground to stand on."

Objectively speaking, he was right. Which made it even more urgent that we find the lost art and return it to the Gardner. Then we'd be heroes, and the humiliated FBI could go stick it. Before they left Lenox, the two agents had said they were looking for Bucky and wanted to get his reaction to his mother's tale. They said they had been unable to locate him and had hoped he would be present at his mother's funeral. They planned on tracking him down at the ball park, where he was expected back at work the following week. My aim was to find him before then, and by now I knew exactly how to obtain his total cooperation – *if* I could somehow meet the incorrigible art thief face to face.

"I'm a big fat liar," Kate said, "and maybe I'll pay a price for that. But so is Father Thigpen. And the question is, why? If he didn't steal the Gardner art, then how come he and those other prevaricating priests in Pittsfield said he was in Vermont on a retreat when he was actually in Boston blabbing to the FBI and chowing down happily at Legal Seafoods? He is in no way in the all clear, as far as I'm concerned."

"Maybe more importantly," I said, "what's the deal with this Sean Cunard, the gallery owner who was attacked and robbed yesterday when we now know Bucky was here in Lenox? It would be an awfully good idea to talk to this guy. Did he know your aunt?"

"I have no idea. Possibly."

"Anyway, it was sculpture that was stolen from him," Timmy pointed out. "Not paintings."

Kate picked up her phone. "I'll check on that. The *Eagle* will have something up."

"We still don't know where Bucky is," I said. "His phone is still off. He must know he's being tracked, though I can only guess how he figured that out. What we do know is, on Thursday night Bucky almost certainly finally learned from a couple of dirty cops in Boston who Miles Tate had become. And it only cost him four hundred dollars' worth of box seat

Sox tickets. Then the next day an art dealer – I said *art dealer* – in Lenox is beaten up and lands in the hospital. What about that?"

Kate said, "The *Eagle* story says Cunard was found last night badly injured and tied up in his gallery. Marcel Descantienne discovered him when he arrived at the gallery around eight p.m. to drop off some new work he had completed. Two of the sculptor's ballerinas had been taken, as well as an undetermined amount of cash. The victim was unable to identify his attacker because he was wearing a ski mask, Cunard told Lenox police. The gallery owner remained in Berkshire Medical Center with injuries that were described as serious but not life-threatening. Cunard said he did not know what object had been used in the assault. But a doctor at BMC said Cunard's injuries were consistent with his having been beaten with something resembling a baseball bat.

CHAPTER 32

"HOW," TIMMY WONDERED, "could Cunard not know what kind of thing he had been beaten with? Was he blindfolded before he was attacked?"

"The paper says he was tied up. Maybe he was blindfolded too."

Timmy raised an eyebrow. "Something here doesn't compute."

I asked Kate what she knew about Cunard. Was he, for instance, a Lenox native?

"I don't think so. He's the only Cunard I know of around here. But he's been in town for quite a while. Art galleries come and go, but the Cunard Gallery has been here for years. I can check with the arts editor at the *Eagle*. He'd know."

Arthur had been out for a stroll, and now he hopped up the steps and sat staring at the screen door.

"Is there a Mrs. Cunard? Any little Cunards that you know of?"

"I'm not aware of any."

"How old a guy would you say he is?"

"Mid-fifties, maybe. Hmm."

Timmy and I also said, "Hmm."

Kate got up and let Arthur into the house.

Resuming her seat and reaching for the white wine, Kate said, "As far back as I can remember, Cunard has represented

Marcel Descantienne. I'm sure he does very well. Marcel has a huge following. Selling metal sculpture can be an iffy proposition, but underfed ballerinas seem to be a sure thing."

"What about Descantienne?" Timmy asked. "What's his story? Where was he in 1990? Is he really French?"

"The paper did a story on him one time. He's from Marseille originally. He married Maude Plank, a woman from an old Lenox family and they have a big house on Cliffwood Street about a mile from here. Sean Cunard isn't that far away, either. He has a place on Old Stockbridge Road with some of Marcel's skinny dancers along his driveway. Marcel is now up in years, and it would be hard for me to imagine he'd be involved in anything shady."

Timmy was having none of that. "What? Old people are never crooks?"

"Marcel's this gnarly grandad you see around town. He reeks of harmlessness."

"So must have Monmouth Khachaturian appeared harmless to the people who didn't know any better."

I said, "It's Cunard who's the right age, and it's Cunard who was robbed and beaten by what could well have been a baseball bat. He's the one I want to know more about."

"That speaks to perhaps telling those FBI guys what we know," Timmy said. "They could delve into Cunard's background with a few strokes on a keyboard."

Kate harrumphed. "Yes, and if the lead I gave them panned out, I'd be rewarded with a formal letter of gratitude from the organization's Boston Field Office. I don't want thank-yous, I don't want a cheesy plaque, or even a big trophy. I want the damn money!"

I stated that that was my goal, too, and checked my phone to see if there was anything new from Strathmore. There wasn't. Had they given up on me and moved on?

"They're saying Cunard has serious injuries," I said, "but they're not saying he's in a coma. If he can talk to the Lenox cops, then he can talk to me. What are the current protocols for visitors at Berkshire Medical Center?"

"I'll have to check." Kate picked up her device again. "At the height of covid, it was no visitors at all for a while. Then mainly just family. It keeps changing. It might also depend on what you're in the hospital for."

"I can be Cunard's cousin Donald from Albany. That should get me in."

"Hospitals," Timmy stated, "often have security people working for them who are firm about the institution's rules and aren't easily fooled. In fact, some of the most suspicious people I've ever known have sat at hospital front desks."

"You are forgetting," I swiftly responded, "my success rate as a liar that is perhaps unparalleled in the history of detective work. It's why one of the world's premiere investigative agencies is currently wooing me and is going to be sorely disappointed if I tell them I am about to come into five million dollars and they can take their job and, like the song says, shove it."

Timmy gave me his gimlet eye. "You'll either succeed at confronting Cunard or you'll land in the Berkshire County Jail."

Before I left for Pittsfield, I checked on Bucky's whereabouts. I was glad to see that he had turned his phone back on, at least for the moment. But he wasn't nearby in the Berkshires. He was back in Boston.

CHAPTER 33

BEFORE I WAS ESCORTED out of Sean Cunard's room by Berkshire Medical Center security, I left my business card on his bedside table and told him to call me when he was ready.

His initial reaction when I'd walked into his room and said, "Hi, Miles, what do you know about what's become of the Gardner Museum art?" was to stare at me wide-eyed and gasp out, "Who *are* you?"

He was wrapped up in dressings galore, including one around his head. He had a couple of impressive shiners, and he was wired up so the nurses could monitor his this and that.

I had shown him my ID, and instead of spinning out one of my usual falsehoods I told Cunard I was working for Mary Costello's niece Kate in an effort to recover the Gardner art treasures and claim the ten-million-dollar reward.

He kept gawking at me while I spoke – saying I knew he was really Miles Tate and I knew he'd somehow snagged the Gardner treasures from Aunt Mary's house and that Bucky Costello had then tracked him down and beaten him with a baseball bat and forced him to turn over the twice-stolen art – and then Cunard pressed the call-a-nurse button again and again until one finally appeared and he croaked out that a crazy person had burst into his room and was harassing him.

When two serious-looking security fellows soon

appeared, I immediately agreed to leave – producing my New York State private investigator's ID but not disclosing the nature of the matter I was currently investigating – and they did not call the police, having been persuaded during a ten-minute interrogation that I was an over-eager professional and not a random lunatic.

Back on Kate's porch, she was excited when I told her and Timmy that I had pretty much confirmed that Sean Cunard was really Miles Tate and it was highly likely that once again Bucky had possession of the Gardner Museum Rembrandts and the Vermeer.

"That's incredible! So the art was here under our noses all the time. Hidden in Cunard's gallery? This is just – wow!"

Timmy was already looking ahead. "But Bucky is back in Boston again. Could that mean *he's* going to return the art to the museum? And claim the reward, for goodness sakes?"

"Oh, God," Kate all but moaned.

"It's possible," I conceded. "The Museum just wants its art back, and they're unlikely to press charges. But they are likely to say to Bucky, *Thank you very much, Mr. Costello. But just out of curiosity, where'd you find this stuff?*"

Timmy laughed. "He could make anything up. *Oh, I came across it in a Salvation Army store.*"

"Somehow," I said, "I don't think any of that is what Bucky has in mind. With his criminal record, he'll know he's likely to be investigated. And he's just smart enough to understand that he won't hold up well under scrutiny."

"Also," Kate pointed out, "he won't want the Costello name besmirched. It would reflect poorly on his morally upstanding late mother."

My phone signaled that I had received a text. I had an idea who it was, and I decided to ignore it for the moment.

"My guess is, Bucky will want to return the art to the museum and cash in to whatever extent he can. But he'll look for an intermediary, a front."

Kate didn't like the sound of that. "Which leaves us out. Oh, no!"

Timmy said, "What if we notify the FBI of what we've learned – I mean you, Donald – and then they work with the museum and set a trap for whenever the front shows up? And they say to the middleman, we know you're in cahoots with Walter Costello – who was one of the original Gardner robbers – and you'd better tell us everything you know or we will fuck you over real good? Wouldn't that work?"

More sandal jiggling from Kate. "I just wonder if we should do anything that provides the museum an excuse to give the reward to anybody besides me."

I agreed we should keep the FBI out of it for the time being. "They will come in handy at some point. But we don't want them charging away and just making everybody who knows anything clam up. They screwed up the Gardner investigation thirty years ago, and let's not give them an opportunity to do it again. They seem to be more interested in grandstanding than crime-solving, but let's not help them out in that regard."

"The FBI is much more professional than it used to be," Timmy opined. "And I think a lot more competent. Anyway, those two agents who showed up said they were going to talk to Bucky when he's back at work at the ballpark next week. So, why not interject ourselves in advance of that, with the off chance that doing so would count for something in what could be some heavy competition for the ten million smackeroos."

Luckily, all this speculative to-ing and fro-ing was soon moot. My phone's ringtone sounded. It was Sean Cunard asking me to return to Berkshire Medical Center. He said he wanted to talk.

CHAPTER 34

"IT MAKES PERFECT SENSE that this guy would actually be Miles Tate," Kate said as we cruised up the Pittsfield-Lenox Road toward the hospital. "It all just fits perfectly with everything else we know about Sean. Which is practically nothing."

She had phoned a couple of other art gallery owners she knew, and none could think of any information they had about Sean Cunard prior to his arrival in the Berkshires three decades earlier. One said he was under the impression Cunard was from the Midwest somewhere, and the other told Kate she thought she recalled Cunard's saying something about coming from Nova Scotia.

As we drove, Kate also made some snide comments about the large new hotels we passed, such as, "That one looks like a container ship with windows. Ugh."

"During my few minutes with him," I said, "Cunard kept saying I was crazy, but he never denied he was Tate."

"And his inviting you back so quickly," Timmy added, "is further proof. This is exciting. I'm feeling as if the Rembrandts and the Vermeer are now practically within our grasp."

"Yeah," I said. "All we have to do is find Bucky and duck when he starts swinging his Ted Williams bat at our heads."

As Kate drove, I checked my phone again. "Bucky is still in Boston. In Back Bay even. Possibly on Newberry Street. What does that mean, if anything?"

Kate muttered, "Returning to the scene of the crime?"

At Berkshire Medical Center, we learned that patients were allowed a maximum of two visitors at a time. Timmy volunteered to wait in the main lobby. On a wall there was a huge painting of cows in a field. We all gazed at it for a moment, wondering what might be hidden behind it.

Kate and I obtained our visitor passes – luckily there had been a shift change and the dinner-hour security officers did not recognize me as a previous trouble-maker – and we rode up to the fourth floor and Cunard's room. He was in a regular unit, not the ICU, telling me he was not too fragile for some persistent questioning.

"You're here," he muttered resignedly as we walked in. "Yeah. Well. Okay, then."

The remains of his dinner were still on a tray in front of him. He had eaten most of the gray meatloaf and mashed potatoes but had left the wilted side salad. The room had two beds in it, and the one closest to the door was unoccupied. The view out the window was of the pretty range of hills west of Pittsfield. If the place had been a hotel, I'd have enjoyed a stay there, while bringing my own food.

Cunard remained heavily bandaged, but none of his limbs was in traction and he was not on oxygen. I could tell that without the blackened eyes and the bruising and swelling on all of his flesh that was visible, he was probably a reasonably fit and possibly quite handsome man in his fifties. Was he hairy or did he have a shaved head? There was no way to tell what was under or not under the extensive wrappings.

Kate and I were both wearing masks, as per BMC regulations. Kate did not extend a hand when she said evenly, "I'm Kate Webster, Mary Costello's niece. I think perhaps you knew my aunt."

Cunard didn't respond at first, so we waited. We had seated ourselves, Kate in the chair provided for Cunard's half of the room. I dragged a chair over from the other section.

"How did you find out about me?" Cunard finally rasped out. His tenor voice was weak and a little shaky but clear enough for us to understand.

"Did you have one of the many keys to Aunt Mary's house that were floating around?" Kate asked.

"It was under a rock by the front steps. She had told me where to find it when I dropped off a plant from Maude Descantienne. It was wintertime, and I couldn't risk leaving the fiddle leaf fig tree outside on the porch."

"So very neighborly of you, Sean. *Miles*, I suppose I should say."

Another pause and a gathering of his thoughts. "I'm just astonished. Really astonished. How did you *do* it?"

I said, "Bucky Costello did it for us, Miles. What did he use on you? His Ted Williams baseball bat?"

He grimaced. "I really believe he would have killed me if I hadn't told him where the paintings were."

"Bucky tracked you down through your phone number. He'd had the number for years without knowing who the number belonged to. When the paintings disappeared from his mother's house, Bucky suspected you right away. But he didn't know what your new identity was until a few days ago. How come he had your number all those years, anyway? It's all pretty peculiar."

Cunard peered back and forth at Kate and me through his puffy face. He said, "I can – I can tell you everything."

"Good," Kate said. "It's why we're here."

"But the thing is…. I mean, here's the thing. How do I get out of this? I mean, what can you offer me in return for the incredibly valuable information I am in a position to impart? I mean – frankly, what's in it for me?"

His chutzpah was impressive. Did he think that if Kate collected the ten-million-dollar Gardner Museum reward, Cunard would collect a 40 percent gallery owner's commission?

"Miles," I said, "I am not the Berkshire County D.A. These are questions someone else will have to answer." Whenever I addressed his as *Miles*, his eyes got wide, and if I'd known which numbers to read on his bedside monitoring device, I'd have probably seen his blood pressure shoot up.

"Oh, God," he moaned. "I am totally fucked!"

"Anyway, Miles, Bucky is going to be caught soon. The FBI is already on his tail. So if you help do what you can to shed light on this whole shoddy fiasco, the better off you'll be. If we can get the paintings back and hand them over to the Gardner, we *will not* share the reward with you, you greedy asshole. But we'll vouch for you as a cooperator who helped us out to some extent. What were you planning to do with the paintings anyway? Return them to the museum and say somebody left them on your doorstep?"

More anguished facial contortions. "Of course not. I was planning on using an acquaintance in Boston who has certain types of connections. He was going to ask the Gardner for a hundred thousand in return for a discreet handover, with no police or other law enforcement involved. The museum would get its great art back, and a few people, myself included, would simply collect a modest finder's fee. I mean, really. What's wrong with that?"

"Does Bucky know who this person is? The middleman who thinks he can do the deal with the museum?"

He nodded. "He made me tell him. He said if I didn't tell him how to do a deal like the one I was planning on, he'd bash my face in. He meant it, too. The guy is totally unhinged."

"Bucky has been unstable since he was a child," Kate said. "Though the violence didn't start until adulthood. It's hard to fathom for those of us who knew him just as a kind of unruly little kid."

"That is strange," Tate/Cunard said through his bandages. "And his mother was such a sweet old gal."

We still didn't get how he knew the Gardner art was hidden behind Mary Costello's cow painting. Then he laid out his remarkable story.

CHAPTER 35

"EARLY THURSDAY MORNING," Cunard began, "Bucky called me."

His voice was still raspy but we heard what we needed to hear. I could see some of the numbers on his monitor start to creep upward, not knowing what they meant.

He went on: "Until then – I know this sounds preposterous – Bucky didn't really know exactly who I was or where I was. I was just a voice on the phone. This was going all the way back to the day after the heist thirty-one years ago when Monmouth unexpectedly, and quite inconveniently, dropped dead."

If Timmy had been there, he might have reflexively crossed himself, but he was down in the hospital lobby looking at a cow painting.

"That day, in March of 1990, Bucky phoned the gallery and asked, what was he supposed to do with the Gardner paintings, which he had in a garbage bag in the backseat of his car? I acted like I had no idea what he was talking about, and I basically told him to screw off. I was totally freaked out by all the police all over the place, and the hysteria, and I just wanted to pretend I didn't know anything whatsoever about what people were already calling the heist of the century.

"But then I gradually began to realize, what the fuck, maybe I can get something out of this after all, especially if it's a reward from the Gardner. Which would have been ironical, but irony was a phenomenon I had long since learned to live with and even appreciate. Anyway, making the mistake of using my own phone, I called Bucky back the next day – his partner Fess-something had fled the scene by this time – and I asked Bucky where was the Gardner art at the present time? I assumed that even though he was a bit of a dim bulb, he had not left it in his car. I told him perhaps I could be helpful in restoring the art treasures to their rightful owner, causing things to settle down.

"But I was too late, Bucky told me. He said he'd been shitting his pants, as he so vividly phrased it, by what Monmouth had gotten him into, and by all the cops and all the media frenzy, and he had taken the art to Lenox, his hometown, and he had hidden it behind the cows. And that was where it was going to stay until the heat was off. *Behind the cows!* Isn't that just choice? I thought, oh, God, the Rembrandts and the Vermeer – Bucky has stuck them in a barn somewhere!"

My peripheral vision took in Kate slowly shaking her head as she learned how some of the world's most renowned and beloved art ended up hidden behind the work of a competent amateur painter in the painter's house on Walker Street in Lenox.

Cunard kept going: "As it happened, with Monmouth's rapacious mistress and his clueless sister closing the gallery instead of letting me keep it going, I needed a fresh start. I was tired, anyway, of being Miles Tate, loser, always somebody's assistant, and I took the Orange Line up to the North End where Monmouth had some rather unsavory acquaintances, and they came up with a new ID for me. I shaved my head and did a few other touch-up-y kinds of things that even fooled the few Boston people who came into the Lenox gallery and said they thought I looked familiar.

"When Monmouth's gallery closed, I actually needed a new ID, because I had helped myself to a few items at his place of business to finance my new beginning. So it was helpful for Miles Tate to be among the unlocatable. I spread the word that Miles had found religion and had gone west.

And I had. Marcel was just beginning to catch on with the art-buying public, and I convinced him that he should let me flog the merchandise while he concentrated on churning out those weird-ass undernourished ballerinas."

I supposed that the arts writer at *The Berkshire Eagle* was used to describing Marcel Descantienne's work differently, but these things were a matter of taste.

"So, meanwhile," Cunard said, "Lenox is a fine place to start my new life, and I am soon making a good living. *And I am convinced that sooner or later I will figure out where the cows are that Bucky has hidden the Gardner art behind.* I can't tell you how many dairy farmers I became friendly with and asked for tours of their operations. There aren't actually a lot of cows in or around Lenox. But, believe me, I've milked most of them – milked them with one eye on the udder and the other eye on any cabinets or other containers in the cows' stalls.

"And then, last year, Maude Descantienne asked me to drop off a plant at Mary Costello's house. When I phoned to work out a time for the drop-off, Mrs. Costello said she'd be away the next day doing environmental work at the service areas on the Mass Pike – at the time, I was puzzled as to what she meant – but that I could just use her house key hidden under a rock by the front steps and place the fig tree on a table in her living room.

"I was struck when I saw the cow painting. Before I left the house, I stood and stared at that painting for the longest time. Then I asked Maude, seemingly in passing, what she knew about Mary Costello, who had such a lovely house. Maude confirmed that Mrs. Costello was an environmentalist of some local note, that her husband, Lewis, a one-time pharmacist, had passed away some years earlier, and that Mrs. Costello had a son, Walter, whom Maude believed lived in Boston. He was rarely seen around Lenox anymore, and, Maude said, the son had some type of criminal past.

"I wondered at that moment if Maude could tell that my pulse was pounding. Because suddenly *I knew!* Finally, after all these may years, I *knew*!"

Kate said, "You're quite the patient man, Miles. And quite the tenacious fellow, too. I mean, good grief!"

I added, "And if the gallery had somehow gone under, you could always have started a dairy farm."

"I knew," Cunard went on, "that it would be wise to wait until Mrs. Costello passed away before I took possession of the art. She might somehow miss it and set something in motion I would not be able to control. I also knew that upon her passing Bucky would get in there and do God knows what with the paintings. I was determined to get there first, and I arranged with Mount Mercy to notify me as soon as Mrs. Costello died. I told them I was her godson and I wished to make a memorial donation to the nursing home in her name. So, on Tuesday I was over there on Walker Street like a shot. The key was under the rock, I got in and out before Bucky arrived, and that was that. I had the Gardner masters in my gallery – above my desk where there's a loose ceiling panel – and it was as huge a coup as any gallery owner could ever hope to achieve in the history of fine art."

I thought of Timmy down in the BMC lobby gazing at the cows, and checking the time on his phone, and wondering what was taking Kate and me so long. I couldn't text him because I was riveted by Tate/Cunard's amazing saga.

"What were you planning to do with the paintings?" Kate asked. "Return them to the Gardner, I hope."

Cunard started to laugh, and then winced from the pain of it, and he took a moment to catch his breath. Then he said, "No. I wasn't going the show up at the museum, missing art in hand. At least, not directly. I won't admit this to anyone but you two. I feel I can be honest with you because I can see you are as addicted to the main chance as I am. And as avaricious. I was planning to fence the art through certain of Monmouth's old unsavory acquaintances in Boston. One of them has since died, but his son is still maintaining the family's North End firm and was definitely interested in involving himself in a transaction that would both add to the family coffers and place him in the good graces of the Boston business and civic establishment."

Kate glowered. "Sean, I just want to pay off my Visa bill. Is that avaricious?"

He ignored that and forged on. "So I actually thought I had gotten away with something. Bucky and I had never actually been introduced, and he still just knew me as a voice and a phone number. But then, damn it, modern technology caught up with me. I had called Bucky periodically over the years trying unsuccessfully to pick up more clues as to where he had hidden the paintings. And of course trying to strike a deal with him for fencing the art and splitting the proceeds. So Bucky had my current phone number in his possession, and that was my mistake. Bucky recently heard that you could track people's phones with certain apps and that if you had friends in certain places you could identify the owners of phones with blocked IDs. And then I was fucked."

"He already suspected," I said, "that it was you who had made off with the art behind the cows. And he found you."

"He not only found me, he showed up Thursday at closing time with a baseball bat. He told me this was a bat Ted Williams once used, and it's still in good shape except for some blood stains, and he is going to bash my brains in with it if I don't hand over the Gardner paintings. I can't very well call the cops, right? At first, I thought I could talk my way out of it. Stall, buy time, and then somehow regroup. I said, oh, somebody else has the paintings. It will take some time and come back next week. That's when he started pounding me. God, I'm bruised all over, I have a concussion, I lost two teeth, and they said they might have to remove my spleen!"

"My cousin was nonviolent as a kid," Kate said. "But now certain things set him off. I guess half a billion dollars' worth of art he thinks is rightfully his is one of them."

"So I told him to stop, and okay, he could have the art, I just needed to be physically able to retrieve it from my office ceiling. I was actually in too much pain by then and could barely move, so Bucky had to get up on my desk and I told him what to do, and he brought the garbage bag down him-self and looked inside to make sure I wasn't tricking him. Then, as if that wasn't enough, he demanded to know who I was planning to fence the paintings with. I thought of making something up, but I knew he'd just come back and kill me. So I told him."

"Smart," I said.

"And then – I could hardly believe my ears – there was *more*."

Kate couldn't help feeling a modicum of sympathy. "Wow."

"He pointed at two of Marcel's newer small ballerinas, and he said, These things are worth money, right? I said, yes, to the right buyers. And he stuck them in the bag with the paintings. Then the bastard demanded cash. I told him I had very little at the gallery, that clients generally paid by check or credit card. That's bullshit, he said, and he said somebody at Fenway Park told him that art buyers and dealers con-stantly dealt in cash to con the IRS, and where was my cur-rency stash hidden? I had to dig some cash out of a shoebox just to get rid of this maniac."

"Bucky is apparently not as stupid as some people say," Kate remarked.

"And then," Cunard/Tate said, looking even more injured, "the guy actually tied me up! I mean, *why*? He knew some-body would find me and I'd have to talk to the police. And that I wasn't going to admit what actually happened, and who attacked me, and why. It was simply – what's the word?"

"Gratuitous?" Kate offered.

"Exactly. What kind of person would do such a thing? It was just lucky Marcel came by a few hours later with new work. I'd probably still be lying on the floor in my office bleeding."

"How much cash did Bucky walk off with?" Kate won-dered.

"Plenty," was all Cunard would say, and winced again.

The big question, though, was the one I asked next. "You were forced to give Bucky the name of the Boston fence you were planning to use. Who is that person?"

Cunard sighed through his swollen lips, and he named a name, recited a phone number, and provided me a brief backgrounder on the late Remo Chicarelli and on his son Jared, present-day proprietor of the family business. Down in the hospital lobby, I found a quiet corner, dialed Jared's number, and left a message.

CHAPTER 36

"I AM THUNDERSTRUCK."

Timmy was agog. On the ride back to Lenox, Kate and I took turns narrating Sean Cunard's wild tale of his thirty-year search for the stolen Gardner art and how he only had it in his possession a few days before Bucky showed up with his baseball bat and made off with it all over again.

"Well, at least," Timmy said, "even if Bucky gets to the fence before we do, we know the art treasures will likely soon be returned to the Gardner safely and, one would hope, relatively undamaged. And that's the most important thing."

Kate, who was driving, glared at Timmy in the rear-view mirror. "Like hell that's the most important thing!"

"Oh. I'm not saying the reward is *un*important. But you know what I mean, Kate."

"Yes. I know what you mean. And what I mean is, I *need* that reward. And I *deserve* it, too. Aunt Mary told *me* where the art was hidden, and she meant for *me* to recover it. Bucky is a – he's a damned criminal. And the idea that he might profit from the return of the art at this point is just wrong, wrong, wrong. We have to stop him, we just *have* to!"

"You're absolutely right," Timmy intoned from the back seat. "All I meant was, having the museum get its Rembrandts back will be such a wonderful thing." I was sure he was keeping an eye on the oncoming traffic, fearful that an agitated

177

Kate might veer into the Pittsfield-Lenox Road's northbound lanes.

"And I can use my five-mil cut," I added. "That is, if I decide not to take a job with Strathmore. Which I'm still mulling over. I have until midnight to decide."

I had checked my texts, and there she was again, Laurel Peaseley: *Just moseying into line of sight to inquire as to your current thinking, Donald, vis a vis joining our elite team, as prestigious in Albuquerque as it is in Asuncion. Please oh-so-kindly respond by the witching hour tonight EDT – fingers and toes crossed!"*

"So, do you think you'll take the Strathmore job?" Kate asked. "How are you tending?"

"I'm tending this way and that way."

"It sounds as if you're doubtful I'll ever collect the reward."

"Somewhat," I admitted. "If the Gardner can get its art back for a lot less than ten million, they will do it. And who can blame them? But Bucky is still in Boston – I checked again five minutes ago – and he might not have located the mob guy whose name Sean gave him. At least, I know Bucky is not back in Belmont. And he basically can't go home until he can tell Janice that his investment paid off hugely and he is returning the four hundred dollars he stole from her underwear drawer."

"Who were you talking to on the phone back at the hospital?" Timmy asked. "Was it the fence? You said Cunard gave you his number."

"I got the guy's voice mail, Jared Chicarelli. I don't know if it'll work, but I put in what amounts to a bid on the art. I'm just hoping Bucky didn't get there first and the art has already slipped through our fingers. Cunard said this guy is sometimes slow in responding to messages, so we'll have to see."

I sensed Kate tense up. She was in the fast lane of the four-lane highway down to Lenox, and she signaled, moved right, and slowed down. I guessed she was losing heart, and

I understood all too well. It seemed there was now only an off chance that the three of us would be the saviors of the Gardner treasures.

Timmy said, "What do you mean by, you put in a bid on the art? Not a cash bid, I assume."

"Nope. I won't be asking for use of your MasterCard, Timothy. What I offered the guy is a deal."

"I'm happy you're in a position to do that. What's the deal?"

Kate swung right onto 7-A, the road toward the middle of Lenox. We'd soon be back at her house – only briefly in my case, if I was lucky.

"The deal is," I said, "that in return for the Gardner art, I won't tell the FBI that Chicarelli obtained the paintings from one of the original thieves, making him an accessory to one of the greatest property thefts of all time. Cunard said the senior Chicarelli was an old-time mob guy, but young Jared is semi-respectable and operates an honest-to-god legitimate art gallery on Newberry Street. His wife was an art history major at Mount Holyoke and basically runs the place, and Jared does a certain amount of money-laundering but mostly stays away from the kind of really dark stuff his pop did in the old days – loan-sharking, truck hijacking, what have you. It was Remo who was going to arrange for Monmouth Khachaturian to fence the Gardner art with his mob contacts in Philadelphia. Jared's wife, the Mount Holyoke alum, will be unlikely to want any of this to be bruited about in the city that calls itself the Athens of America. So I do believe I can deal with this guy – if, as I say, it's not too late."

Timmy and Kate were both quiet for a long minute.

As she pulled into her driveway, Kate said, "That all sounds to me – what's the word I'm looking for?"

Timmy helped her out. "Tenuous?"

But Bucky was a flake and I wasn't. So my ploy didn't seem to me entirely hopeless. It was merely – Timmy was often the man with the *mot juste* – tenuous.

CHAPTER 37

"BUCKY AND FESS TETLOW were right about one thing," Kate said. "Miles Tate was gay, and as Sean Cunard he still is."

Timmy was just back from driving into the center of town to pick up another pizza and a Greek salad, and I while I waited for Jared Chicarelli to call back, Kate had been on the phone with friends she thought might know more about Cunard.

"Sean is not currently partnered – in fact, never has been, I'm told, while he's been in Lenox – but my gay friend Stanley says he knows guys Sean has hooked up with online, and before Covid hit, Sean sometimes turned up at a gay bathhouse in Providence."

"I guess," I said, "he couldn't risk having a close relationship with somebody who'd be curious about Sean's life before the age of twenty-six or whatever it was."

Kate had placed some plates and napkins on the kitchen table, and Timmy was opening the pizza box, further releasing its intoxicating aromas. It was only Arthur, dozing next to the microwave, who was indifferent to the fragrance. He seemed to be interested only in food that came out of a can.

"I suppose," Timmy said, "if Sean wanted a relationship, he could have gone online and advertised for a fellow crook. *Seeking power bottom, love to cuddle, art theft experience a plus.*"

"Or maybe," Kate mused, "Sean simply isn't the marrying kind. Gay people like that still exist."

"Anyway," I added, "a history of shape-shifting can never be good for a marriage, straight or gay. It would definitely affect the level of trust."

"Though it's a wonder," Timmy said, "that any of us who are gay ever learned to trust, or ever earned the right to be trusted. We spent so much of our young lives lying to ourselves, or lying to other people, or both. I know I practically had to learn how loving relationships are supposed to work from an Arthur Frommer guide."

Kate explained that her friend was somewhat different. "Stanley told me he knew he was gay from about the age of eight. And so did everybody else, on account of his mannerisms. He's extremely – what's the word?"

"Sissified," Timmy recited. "It's a blessing as a medium for self-awareness, but it used to be it could also get you beaten up every day of the week. Still does in a lot of places, I'm sure."

"Stanley says being that way did cause some problems. But it also meant he had some enjoyable episodes with certain supposedly straight members of the North Adams High School football team behind the bleachers late on summer nights."

"Feigning being butcher-than-thou to all of Poughkeepsie and to myself, I missed out on such events," Timmy lamented.

"It's interesting," Kate said, "that Bucky and Fess picked up on Miles Tate being gay. Or was it just because he worked in an art gallery and not a foundry?"

"That's the likely explanation," I said. "Timothy, Fess and Bucky would probably decide you were gay because you don't pick your pizza up with your fingers, you eat it with a knife and fork."

"Yes, like Donald Trump. And they'd probably think you were straight because you pick yours up with your large, hairy hands, like Mike Lindell, the My Pillow guy."

Timmy and I both laughed, and after a few seconds Kate

did, too.

"I'm kind of sorry that Cunard, the conniving art thief, is gay," Timmy said. "It's bad for the brand."

"Jeffrey Dahmer was one of our people," I pointed out, "and the Supreme Court still ruled in favor of gay marriage."

"Dahmer wasn't a plaintiff in that case, as I recall."

"Anyway, it might not come out that Cunard is really Miles Tate and he stole the Gardner paintings from Mary Costello's house and kept them hidden in his gallery for four days. If part of what I have in mind for recovering the paintings from Bucky works, only Bucky himself might have to take the fall in this. And then, only in a limited way."

Timmy and Kate were both listening carefully between bites of Greek salad and pepperoni and mushroom pizza.

"The main goals here," I said, "are threefold. One is to get the *Storm On the Sea of Galilee* back into its frame at the Gardner Museum. Another goal is for you, Kate, to obtain the ten-million-dollar reward. The third aim is for me to get my cut of the proceeds so I can tell Strathmore, thanks but no thanks. I have another four hours before I have to make that decision and let Strathmore know what it is. I could ask for a day's extension, and they might give it to me – they do seem to want me on what they enjoy calling their *elite team*. But I think the message I left with Jared Chicarelli might be enticing enough for him to want to deal. Provided, of course, that he has possession of the Gardner paintings, or at least soon expects to have them."

After a moment, Timmy said, "*Threefold.* That's a word *I* might use."

"Normally, you are better at organizing your thoughts than I am. But the current situation here is beginning to take on a clarity that I can't but help grasp and, I think, bring a good enough amount of control over. I have to tell you, the more I think about exactly what we're faced with here, the more confident I'm starting to feel."

It was not more than a minute later that my cell phone rang. It was, in fact, Jared Chicarelli calling back. He told me he would be glad to talk to me if I could meet him in Boston around eleven o'clock after he finished a dinner engagement. He said he hoped I would not be too disappointed with what he had to tell me.

CHAPTER 38

"YOU COULD HAVE JUST told me this on the phone," I said. "Why make me drive across the entire state of Massachusetts for this information that is quite interesting to me but not at all what I badly wanted to hear?"

We were seated at the bar at La Nonnina, the Newberry Street restaurant Chicarelli owned. The late-evening diners were finishing up their porchetta di Ariccia and pasta al nero di seppia, and some were ordering desserts and espresso. Chicarelli had just dined with a group of friends, he told me, and he had stayed on to meet me.

"I was curious as to what this is all about," he said. "I mean, the missing Gardner Museum art? That's quite the big fucking deal. First, Sean Cunard calls me and purports to have possession of it – and then he didn't – and then you and Sean thought *I* had possession of it – or I was about to take possession of it – and naturally I am quite interested in knowing what the hell this is all about."

Slender and dark, he was as sleek as the interior of his eatery, with the same mix of shiny surfaces and comforting shadows. He seemed to have recessed lighting in his eye sockets. His suit made my made-in-Bangkok, chewed-by-rodents funeral outfit – I still had it on – look like the schmatta someone of my current low financial status would parade around in naively, as if the way one presented oneself to the world meant nothing at all.

"But you did say," I said, "that Bucky Costello had been in to see you at your gallery. Did I somehow misunderstand your description of his visit?"

He sipped from a shapely glass containing an amber fluid. I was drinking Sam Adams out of a bottle to calm me down. What *was* going on here?

"Bucky Costello, the art thief. Yes, he came into the gallery this afternoon. Normally I would not be there. My wife Ellen oversees the gallery, it being her passion. But today she was taking our son Lance to visit his maternal grandmother at her retirement community in Lexington. So I was minding the store, so to speak."

"Uh huh. And Bucky identified himself using his real name?"

"He said he had once done a job of some type for a business associate of my late father's. And someone who had once worked for this business associate, so-called, had given him my name and the gallery address. I knew he meant Sean."

"Cunard had alerted you."

"Sean and I do business from time to time. Moving art around, what have you. Sean did not advise me that you might also come calling. But here you are, and I have to say I am intrigued."

"I'm intriguing when called upon to be so."

"Costello said he had some art to sell that he thought someone with my contacts might be interested in."

"With your contacts? What's that mean?"

Chicarelli sipped some of his beautiful liquid. "For a second or two, the idea went through my head, could this be a set-up?"

"You might think that."

"But then I thought, hell, this guy is such a jamoke that he can't possibly be some type of law enforcement. And anyway, Sean sent him to me, and Sean is hardly someone who would be party to trickery of that nature."

"No, not of that nature."

"I said to Costello, what's the art you have to sell? And I waited for his big Gardner announcement."

"You were on pins and needles."

"He had this garbage bag with him, and he reached in and pulled out these two two-foot-high steel statuettes of ballerinas. They were like something Degas might have considered doing and then thought better of it. The dancers were grinning, but they looked as if they could've used a couple of arancini to fatten them up."

I'd had pizza earlier in Lenox, but the aromas wafting out of La Nonnina's kitchen were doing a job on me, and two arancini would have hit the spot. I swallowed some more beer.

"He stole those things from the man who sent him to you. Costello's middle name is Chutzpah."

"I understood that right away. And with no mention of the Gardner paintings whatsoever, I thought, how the fuck do I get rid of this stupido?"

"Deciding what to do must have been easy."

"It was. He wanted a thousand for each ballerina. I offered him four hundred for the pair, and he took it and left. I've got the dancers stashed in the back of the gallery out of sight. Ellen will wonder how they got there, and I'll concoct some story."

"It's not a type of art she goes for?"

"She likes all types. Just so it's good. She was an art history major at Mount Holyoke. We met when I was a junior up the road at Hampshire College."

I just didn't get it. "And Bucky never mentioned the stolen Gardner paintings? The Rembrandts and the Vermeer and all the rest of those great works?"

Chicarelli's dark eyes brightened. "Christ, I wish he had. What's the reward these days for the return of the paintings? Five million?"

"Ten."

"And how, if I may ask, did this low-grade moron come into possession of the Gardner art? Or at least believe that he had?"

I told Chicarelli the whole story. What was to lose? Why not tell him? Maybe he'd come up with some idea of where Bucky might have turned to next, in order to fence the art.

Chicarelli was rapt as I laid out the saga. When I got to the part about Monmouth Khachaturian, Chicarelli said, "Oh, sure. That sounds right. Pop knew him. I'm not at all surprised."

When I finished telling the story of how two shnooks from the Berkshires pulled off the greatest art heist in modern history, Chicarelli stared down into his heartbreakingly beautiful glass of whatever it was. Then he looked up and said, "So where do you think the paintings are now?"

I just swigged more beer.

CHAPTER 39

"I'M SO SORRY," I told Kate and Timmy. "Chicarelli was as perplexed about the whole thing as I am. He asked me where I thought I would go from here, and I said damned if I know. Bucky is acting totally irrationally, making it all but impossible to know what on Satan's blue earth the guy is doing. It is confounding."

It was just past two in the morning, and we were back at Kate's kitchen table. I had told them the gist of my findings by phone, and they had waited up for me for a more comprehensive depressing report.

"How," Timmy asked, "can you be sure Chicarelli wasn't lying? We might tune in CNN in the morning and see *Breaking News – Boston art gallery owner and fettuccini purveyor returns art treasures to museum and collects multi-million-dollar reward.* The guy is from a mob family, after all. How trustworthy can anybody with that type of background be?"

I told him his skepticism was understandable. "But," I said, "why would he lie to me? He could have just said, yeah, he has the lost art, and he plans to return it to the Gardner and collect any amount they are willing to fork over. He could have said, *Too bad, sucker. I win, you lose.* That's mob-speak. Not, *Oh, this is interesting, I wonder what in heaven's name it is all about?*"

He stifled a yawn. "Well, if that's your assessment."

"Granted, this Chicarelli is of a different generation from his dad's. He doesn't get his jollies from knee-capping the competition verbally or literally. He's from the generation that went to Mount Holyoke and Hampshire, and he's subtler. But he as much as admitted to me – and said it quite casually – that he deals in art whose ownership origins are opaque. So it would be a point of pride for Chicarelli to admit trading in a missing Rembrandt or two. I think he was telling the truth."

Kate was also having trouble staying awake. Unlike her cat, who was on the kitchen counter snoring.

"It sounds," Kate said blearily, "as if you've all but given up on catching Bucky and retrieving the paintings. Or am I not hearing you correctly?"

"It's not looking promising. I'm sorry, Kate. I checked my Spy-oh-my a while ago while I was on the pike and Bucky was in Belmont, maybe back with Janice. I'm guessing he returned the four hundred dollars he stole from her either with the money he grabbed from Sean Cunard or the cash Jared Chicarelli paid for the two ballerinas. Anyway, I thought about turning around and heading for Belmont, and it's a good thing I didn't. Because when I checked again a little while later, Bucky was headed north on I-93. Where was he going? New Hampshire? Maine? Any idea what that might mean?"

Kate snorted. "God, no. Not a clue."

"Maybe," Timmy said, "Sean Cunard will have some idea of what a Plan B might be for Bucky. I mean, if Chicarelli wasn't going to work out – which he didn't."

"I can ask him. But he seemed sure Chicarelli would be the best man to do a deal with the museum."

Kate looked frazzled and sounded disgusted. "What do you think it was about Chicarelli that made Bucky change his mind about him? He sounds to me like exactly the kind of high-toned scoundrel Bucky would be willing to place his confidence in."

"Like Monmouth Khachaturian," Timmy added. "A Newberry Street swell. A man with what Meyer Wolfsheim called *gonnegtions*. Not that Wolfsheim was anywhere near as slick as this Chicarelli seems to be."

Kate perked up. "In *Gatsby*, Wolfsheim was based on the mob guy who fixed the 1919 World Series. Bucky would have been impressed by that. Not that the Red Sox were involved."

"Who was it?" Timmy wondered. "It was the White Sox who threw the series. But who actually won?"

Kate was apparently too worn out, physically and otherwise, to look it up, and I got out my phone.

"It was the Reds. Cincinnati. This was before they changed their name to the Redlegs in the 1950s so people wouldn't think they were communists."

We sat quietly for a couple of minutes. None of us was eating or drinking. Kate had said something about getting out some weed she'd picked up at the pot shop over in Lee, but she hadn't gotten around to it.

Finally, Timmy said, "I guess at this point there's really only one thing we can do."

"I know," Kate said. "Call those FBI guys."

"Yep."

"And hope that they can catch Bucky and retrieve the paintings. And maybe convince the Gardner to throw a few rupees our way because it was our information that led to the much desired outcome for the museum."

"Those agents won't be happy," I said, "that we lied through our teeth to them earlier today. But the important thing is, they'll be able to call a press conference and wave the Rembrandts around. And they'll have gotten over any huffiness they might have felt about us at first. Trout and Brisbane will ride on a float down Boylston Street, waving *Storm on the Sea of Galilee,* as thousands cheer."

"And you, Kate," Timmy said, "will get that nice thank-you note from the Boston Field Office."

"Jesus. There goes the ten mil. I mean – oh shit."

"I'm sorry, Don," Timmy said, "that you're unlikely to collect your five mil. But don't worry about money. Really. We'll figure that out."

"I'm not worried. Not at all. Before I left Boston just

before midnight, I texted Strathmore. I said I'd take the job."

Kate dragged herself off her chair and went to look for her weed stash.

CHAPTER 40

SUNDAY MORNING, TIMMY and I slept in. When I woke up a little after ten, Timmy was still conked out. Before I got out of bed, I checked my phone to see where Bucky was. He was stationary in the town of Woburn, along I-93 about ten miles north of Boston. What was he doing there? And what was Woburn? I wasn't even sure how to pronounce it.

Should I speed across the state again and hope Bucky was still in the mysterious Woburn and then hope I might spot him somewhere? I wasn't up to it.

I hauled myself out of bed, got into some pants and a T-shirt, and made my way down the hall to the bathroom. The door was shut. Kate? One of her B&B guests?

I knew there was a bathroom downstairs, and I padded down the steps barefooted. I did what I needed to do, then had a quick look in the kitchen. Kate, awake and alert, was just coming in the side door carrying the *New York Times*.

"Donald, good morning, good morning, good morning. How'd you sleep?"

"Well enough. You?"

"Definitely *not* well enough. The Grishams will be down shortly, I think. They'll need their Sunday *Times*. I just ran into town."

"Can't they get it on their devices? Timmy and I do."

"They're older, and only the print edition is real to them."

I smelled coffee brewing, and when Kate offered me a mug of it, I thanked her mightily and took it.

"Why would Bucky be in Woburn, do you think? Am I pronouncing it correctly?" I had said *WOE-burn.*

"It's sort of *WOO-burn,*" she said. "With the *woo* as in *book.* Bucky is in Woburn? I have no idea why."

"Are there – I don't know – art galleries there?"

"I'd have to check."

I sat down at the kitchen table, imbibed, borrowed Kate's phone, and looked up *art galleries Woburn MA.* There were three, plus dozens more if you included *near Woburn* in the search. Boston's Museum of Fine Art got plenty of play, as of course did the Isabella Stewart Gardner Museum.

On their websites, the three galleries in Woburn all looked respectable enough, but how would I know if any of them wasn't?

A woman I took to be Kate's paying guest Phyllis Grisham strolled into the room, greeted us cheerily, and introduced herself to me. My pre-shower dishevelment didn't seem to faze her. When she asked me if I had stayed at Kate's B&B before, Kate explained that I was not a B&B guest but a friend. Mrs. Grisham – short, compact, stylish, about seventy-five – grinned and winked at me. When Timmy appeared, she was going to be confused.

"It was a quiet night in Lenox last night," Mrs. Grisham said, eagerly accepting a mug of coffee from Kate. "We had dinner with some city friends, Ruth and Nate Snyderman, and some friends of theirs, and Church Street was a good deal quieter last night than it was on Friday night. Did you hear about the art gallery robbery? I mean, in Lenox! Who'd've thought?"

"We heard about that," Kate said. "Everybody in town is knocked for a loop."

Mrs. Grisham perched on a stool by the counter and Arthur looked up at her. *Who are you?*

"The Snydermans said they heard it had something to do with drugs. Almost fifty thousand dollars in cash was taken.

194

Who keeps that kind of cash around unless it's drug dealers?"

"That would be hard to believe about Sean Cunard. He's always been a kind of model of respectability in Lenox. What else did the Snydermans hear?"

"That Marcel Descantienne was somehow involved. His wife, too. What's her name? Miriam?"

"Maude. She was Maude Plank, one of the Cliffwood Street Planks."

"I hope she has more meat on her bones than those anorexic ballerinas do that her husband makes. Those things give me the heebie-jeebies. The Snydermans' friends, the Kramers, think they're fabulous. They even own one. When they said that, Leon and I looked at each other and we just kept our mouths shut. Which is not easy for me," Mrs. Grisham added, and laughed.

Kate had picked up some fresh muffins in town and was fixing them on a platter along with a small plate of butter and a dish of fig jam.

"I hope," Mrs. Grisham went on, "Descantienne didn't use live models for the little ones. Someone would've had to call Child Protective Services."

Her husband appeared, looking chipper and recently parboiled. A man of about his wife's age, Leon Grisham seemed comfortable in his weekend-in-the-Berkshires pressed slacks and linen jacket. His wife filled him in on what we'd been discussing, and he said, "If the gallery owner was selling fentanyl, I'd say he got what he deserved. I understand he's in the ICU with brain injuries and two smashed kneecaps. If he ever walks again, it will be a miracle, the Snydermans said."

"The Kramers said they thought Cunard was related to the Sacklers," his wife added.

Leon Grisham shook his head. "That's just because he was selling fentanyl. Anyway, how would the Kramers know who the guy was related to? They're the types who pick up stuff up on the internet and believe what fits their predetermined ideas of who somebody is. For all anybody knows, Cunard could be nothing more than some Gatsby-like self-invented hustler related to nobody in particular."

"Right," his wife went along. "And maybe it isn't even illicit drugs he's dealing in, now that I think about it. I mean, an art gallery as a drug den? Really? People would notice who's coming and going and put two and two together. I'm betting they'll find out it's stolen art Cunard is retailing. That would explain the huge amount of cash the robber took. A hundred thousand, or whatever it was."

"That would make a kind of sense," Mr. Grisham agreed. "Phyllis, you're right on the money, as usual."

"I don't suppose it would be on a huge scale, though, this being Lenox. I mean, we're not talking museum-quality stolen art moving through your quiet little burg here. The Gardner Museum Rembrandts, or like that."

Just then Timmy walked into the room, spiffily turned out and, like Leon Grisham, freshly scrubbed. He gawked at Mrs. Grisham for a long moment, and said, "Gee whiz, what am I missing here?"

CHAPTER 41

AFTER THE GRISHAMS LEFT to take a walk around town and look in at shops and non-scandalous art galleries, Kate phoned a reporter friend at the *Eagle* and asked what was new on the Sean Cunard robbery. Not much, the reporter said. There were plenty of crazy rumors going around – a Norman Rockwell had been taken, plus over a million in cash – but the police were somewhat perplexed by the whole thing. They still couldn't understand why Cunard had been unable to tell them what weapon had been used to beat him with. The attacker had been wearing a ski mask, but Cunard should have been able to see what that thing was pounding him over the head.

"After we tell the FBI what we know," Kate said to Timmy and me, "they'll talk to the Lenox cops, who are going to be extremely annoyed that we kept everything we knew from them. They're out there now trying to solve Lenox's crime of the decade – maybe of the century – and we know exactly what happened and we're keeping it to ourselves. This will not go down well."

"But," Timmy quickly retorted, "they will be in no position to complain. When you went to the department with news of the Walker Street break-in and the missing Gardner paintings – the Gardner art treasures, for goodness sakes! – you got the brush-off. They said, oh, crazy old Mary Costello

– pshaw, just you never mind, Mrs. Webster, that whacky story can't possibly be true. So I am guessing that when some version of the truth comes out, the Lenox Police Department will know enough to keep its mouth shut."

We were back out on the porch on a magnificent June Sunday morning. Arthur was on his milk crate, and all was right with the world.

I said, "Maybe Sean will get them off the hook by confessing to at least a few untoward items, if not the entire blood-curdling schemata. When I talked to him a while ago, he didn't sound ready to confess to anything. But when the FBI enters the picture and violations of federal law are spoken of, Sean's intransigence could soften."

Half an hour earlier, I had phoned Cunard at Berkshire Medical Center to get his take on Bucky's showing up at Jared Chicarelli's gallery and never mentioning the Gardner paintings. Cunard was as dumbfounded as Chicarelli was, and as I remained. I had also asked Cunard if he knew of anybody in the town of Woburn who might act as a middleman between Bucky and the museum, and he said no, he didn't. Nor did he have any idea of who Bucky might turn to next.

"It's not that I'm unappreciative of all your great efforts," Kate said, "but it's a fact that when this is over – whatever *over* might turn out to mean – you'll head on back to Albany. And I'll stay here and have to deal with the local constabulary probably for the rest of my life. So even if they are neutralized, so to speak, I think I can expect their attitude toward me to remain cool."

"It would help," Timmy said, "if you could still somehow lay your hands on the ten million dollars. That would earn you a type of respect around Lenox that would count for a lot."

They both looked over at me. I felt more helpless than ever, more pathetically useless. I said, "Yeah. The money would make a difference. But at this point it does appear to be beyond our reach. Unless there's something we're missing here. Some clue to Bucky's thinking that is eluding us, and if we just thought harder, or got lucky, maybe, maybe ..."

Kate perked up a bit. "There's still Father Thigpen. I mean, what's really going on there?"

Timmy and I sat listening and choosing not to dash Kate's hopes too abruptly.

"It's true," she went on, "that Thigpen is the one who alerted the FBI. But he is still on the lam, or so it seems. We should check on that."

"It wouldn't hurt," Timmy uttered halfheartedly.

"It sure seems as if he is up to his clerical collar in this in some very weird way. Why else would those priests in Pittsfield lie about his whereabouts? Why would they cover for him? You said yourself, Donald, that the priest you spoke to, that Father Moyer, seemed to know all about the Gardner paintings and about Father Thigpen going to the feds."

"He might have told them," I pointed out, "about your aunt's confession and what he learned about the hidden paintings. And how he planned to notify the FBI."

Kate sat up. She knew she was onto something. "But then, why not just say he was in Boston on an important matter? Why make up some lie about him being on a religious retreat in Vermont? Anyway, he's away, they said, for ten days. It doesn't take ten days to walk into the Federal Building and tell an agent there what Thigpen knows. No, that guy is up to something, and I have a feeling that if we can find out what that something is, we'll still have a shot at the Gardner ten mil."

What Kate said made a modicum of sense. I asked her if there was a discreet way to find out things about Thigpen and also about Father Moyer and the other priests in their Pittsfield rectory.

"I know somebody who's a big donor to Catholic charities in Pittsfield. Charles Grady knows his way around the parishes, and if there's anything funny going on among the Pittsfield Catholic clergy, he'd have heard about it. We should talk to Charles."

"Sounds good."

"And let's not waste any time."

Kate got on her phone. She reached famously-well-informed Charles Grady on his cell while he was playing the sixth hole on the golf course at the Pittsfield Country Club. When she told him she needed to know a few things about a Father Michael Thigpen, Grady paused. Then he said perhaps he could drop by after his golf game and he and Kate could have a chat.

CHAPTER 42

ACCORDING TO MY SPY-OH-MY, Bucky was back on I-93 heading south toward Boston again, having departed Woburn, when Charles Grady arrived on Kate's porch mid-afternoon. The sky had clouded over, but the air was almost tropical as we lolled next to Arthur. Chardonnay was produced for Timmy and Kate. I had picked up some Sam Adams for me, and Grady accepted a bottle also.

After Grady expressed his condolences over the passing of Kate's Aunt Mary and some small talk was exchanged, the visitor asked Kate how come she wanted to know more about Father Michael Thigpen? She replied that Father Mike had given Mary Costello her last rites and Kate had heard some things about the priest that piqued her interest.

"What kind of things?"

"You go first, Charles. What kind of things do you think I might have heard?"

Grady was a man in his sixties who Kate had told us owned a shoe outlet on the north side of Pittsfield. Silver-maned and apple-cheeked, he looked comfortably at home in his golf shoes and sporty outfit.

"The priesthood is changing," Grady said conversationally. "Keeping up with the times. I'm sure you know that."

"Yes," Kate said. "I'm not as involved in the church as I was growing up. In fact, not really at all. But I do read a couple of newspapers."

"The priest-pedophile scandals were one thing. And let's hope we've seen the last of all that."

"Yes, let's."

"But healthy, adult, intimate relationships for priests might eventually be in the offing. Unless marriage is allowed, it's hard to see how the Vatican can continue to recruit sufficient numbers of clergy to keep the churches functioning."

"I've read about that."

"Same-sex relationships are another matter, of course. That could take a while."

Kate had introduced me and Timmy as a couple, and he was telling us something we knew and he knew we knew.

"Meanwhile," Grady went on, "the church often overlooks priests having relationships with other priests. If the Diocese butted in on these unions, the priesthood would wither away even faster than is presently the case."

I could see in Kate's eyes a dawning realization of where this was heading. She said, "Oh dear."

"So, is that what you heard about Father Thigpen?" Grady asked. "That he's gay? And he has a long-time partner who is also a priest in Pittsfield?"

"No, I did not hear that. Oh, for heaven's sake."

"But I'm guessing it's nothing that's going to knock the wind out of you."

She laughed lightly. "Not for any reason I can really go into. It's just that – Donald here was trying to get in touch with Father Mike. And a priest in Pittsfield told Don the Father was on a retreat in Vermont. And then somebody saw him in a restaurant in Boston. And – there was some other stuff, too."

Grady chuckled. "Father Mike and Father Raphael are well-liked, and I know the other priests protect their privacy. Somebody saw them in Boston? They were probably heading to or from Provincetown, where they spend a week every year. They're friends of Varla Jean Merman, and they attend her hilarious drag act at the Art House on Commercial Street nearly every night. My wife and I were in attendance one night and saw them there, and we all said hello. They were not, of course, in priestly garb at the time."

"Well," Kate said. "This is – fascinating."

"It sounds as if you suspected Father Mike of something else. May I ask what that something else might have been?"

Kate's sandaled foot was jiggling up a storm. "I actually thought he might have – hold onto your hat, Charles – stolen some art from Aunt Mary's house."

"Where in the world did you ever get that idea?"

That's when I jumped in. "We all got this stupid notion in our heads. It was after Mrs. Costello's passing, and some art in her house turned up missing. But it was all a total misunderstanding."

"Did it have something to do with the art robbery at the Sean Cunard Gallery?" Grady asked. "Lenox seems to have become the art-robbery capital of New England this year. Though I can't imagine Father Mike would have had anything to do with that one, either."

We all stared at Grady. Timmy said, "You know, Varla Jean Merman advertises herself as the illegitimate daughter of Ernest Borgnine and Ethel Merman. But Ernest Borgnine and Ethel Merman were actually married to each other. It's a bit confusing. But I suppose not all that important."

Grady took this in but seemed to have no opinion about it. Soon, he finished his beer and said he needed to get home and attend to lawn work while Mrs. Grady did some gardening. Kate thanked him for the clarification as to Father Thigpen's semi-secret gay life, and we all reassured Grady that we would not broadcast this interesting-to-us but maybe problematical-in-some-quarters information far and wide. Or at all.

After Grady drove away, Timmy said, "Kate, I had been wondering, would anyone ever rid you of that turbulent priest? You, and Don, and me, too. The answer turned out to be yes, and it didn't take four knights to do the job the way it did for James II. Charles Grady appeared on the scene to carry out the grisly task."

"I'm embarrassed," Kate said, "that I suspected this apparently decent man of all sorts of machinations and intrigue."

"When all he wanted was a degree of privacy. And some companionship that included physical affection. And presumably a bit of harmless hoochie-coochie from time to time."

"But of course," Kate said gloomily, "now we're just back where we started. Father Thigpen, the exemplary citizen who notified the authorities that the lost Gardner art had been hidden in Aunt Mary's house – that guy is now totally off the hook. But us? We are as hopelessly lost as we ever were."

"Maybe not," I said, examining my phone. "Bucky seems to be back with Janice in Belmont. And he's not on the move at all."

CHAPTER 43

BLAIR TURKELSON, CEO OF Strathmore Investigations, phoned to tell me how pleased he was that I would soon be joining the company team. He was emailing me a contract that I was to sign and return. He said a possible first assignment might be to find out who had stolen six truckloads of bricks from a client in Utica. I asked him if Strathmore's Asuncion office had any jobs coming up that were more interesting. When he seemed confused, I had to explain that I had said that in jest. Turkelson laughed heartily.

His email with the contract soon arrived. I saved it and thought, I'll take care of this a little later.

Kate had Agent Glenn Trout's FBI business card with his supposed phone number on it. But when she called Sunday late afternoon, she was routed to someone else at the Boston Field Office, a Special Agent Bart MacArthur.

"He didn't know what I was talking about," she told Timmy and me after her call. "Here I am phoning in with reliable information on the Gardner Museum art heist – one of the FBI Boston office's most explosive cases in the last fifty years – and I have to explain to this guy that that's a thing, and it is a thing he should be extremely interested in."

"This is not encouraging," Timmy said.

I fell back on the easy answer. "It's the weekend. You might have to try them tomorrow after nine or ten."

"The guy said he would notify Special Agent Trout of my call and of the additional information I said I had, following up on Agent Trout's interview with me yesterday in Lenox. So maybe Trout will call back tonight. If he gets the message, that is."

Timmy said, "Why are they all called *special* agents? None of them ever seems to be anything less. *How do you do? I'm Ordinary Agent Cosmo Tenafly, and this is my colleague, Humdrum Agent Duane T. Farquar.* I wonder what the history is of that *special* adornment?"

"No doubt something to do with Hoover," I theorized.

"And why are they always men?" Kate wanted to know. "I suppose there are female agents. But not working on this case. Why?"

"Women are better at spotting male liars," Timmy said. "You'd think they would have figured that out."

"It's true. We have so much experience."

"And you ladies are so cunning and accomplished at lying because of that experience," I added. "I was so impressed by the way you really put one over on Trout and Brisbane after the funeral yesterday. All that bullshit about Aunt Mary being so batty that nobody should take anything she said seriously. That was really quite a performance."

Kate studied me. "You're saying that women learn from men to be expert liars? That's novel."

"Yes," Timmy said, giving me a look. "Give women some credit for figuring out on their own that mendacity can be put to worthwhile purposes."

"For myself," Kate said with a strange little half smile, "I can tell you that I have always been uncomfortable even with the small social lie. *I can't come to the dinner party with your boring in-laws because I'm having a colonoscopy that day.* I try hard not to do even that. But with bankruptcy just around the corner for me, dangle ten million dollars in front of my eyes and I'll lie like Trump."

"Though much more convincingly," in Timmy's stated opinion.

In my line of work, I lied a lot, and I sat there on Kate's porch wondering why it came so naturally to me. Because I was a man? Because I was gay and, like Timmy, spent much of my youth throwing people off the scent of my depravity?

All this speculation and pointless palaver soon became moot, however. Just after six o'clock, Special Agent Glenn Trout called Kate back. Timmy and I listened as Kate apologized to Trout and admitted that she had purposely "left a few things out" during her interview with the two Boston agents the previous day.

This time she told the fed that Father Thigpen's account of Mary Costello's confession was all true. That Bucky had stolen the Gardner masterpieces in 1990 and had hidden them in his mother's living room. And that soon after her passing he had found a way to retrieve the paintings – Kate chose to let Sean Cunard off the hook for the time being – and Kate believed that Bucky now had possession of the art – or at least knew where it was located – and that he was most likely at home in Belmont prior to returning to work as a groundskeeper at Fenway Park on Monday morning.

Timmy and I couldn't hear them, but Agent Trout then seemed to have a few questions for Kate. To most of these questions, she answered, "I don't know" or "I have no way of knowing that." But she was able to provide one important piece of information. She retrieved Mary Costello's little Hallmark address book with the floral-pattern cover, and she gave the FBI man Bucky's current home address in Belmont.

Kate added, "Bucky lives with his girlfriend, whose name is Janice Nestor. She works as a waitress at the Friendly's in Belmont."

After Kate hung up, saying Agent Trout appreciated Kate's "coming clean," she said, "I felt bad about bringing Janice into it. I'm sure she is totally innocent in this entire horrible fiasco."

Timmy said, "At least she will have gotten her four hundred dollars back before the feds move in – when? Tonight or tomorrow?"

"They'll probably have to get a warrant to search Bucky's apartment," I pointed out. "So I'd say probably tomorrow."

"A warrant based on what?" Timmy asked. "Kate's tale about her barmy aunt? I'm not so sure about that."

"No," I said, "based on Kate's report, but also on the report to the FBI by Father Michael Thigpen. In Boston, a Catholic priest's word is still the coin of the realm. Even if the particular priest is gay as a birthday piñata, the average Boston judge is likely to give him the benefit of the doubt."

CHAPTER 44

MONDAY MORNING, TIMMY drove my car back to Albany so he could go to work. He had called ahead to Assemblyman Lipschitz's office and was assured nothing pressing was on the day's schedule. Albany was still preoccupied – enthralled even – with the Andrew Cuomo commotion. The governor had been #MeToo-ed up to his hairline and was thrashing about in an attempt to remain in office, but his political future was looking more and more hopeless. Meanwhile, not much else at the Capitol was getting done.

Bucky Costello seemed to be going back to work, too. He had spent the night at home in Belmont, apparently, and then was on the move at 8 a.m. in the direction of Fenway Park in Boston's Fens neighborhood. He no longer felt the need to shut off his phone. Why was that?

I had also been provided the opportunity for gainful employment, although I dawdled. I didn't make a conscious decision to postpone signing and returning the Strathmore contract. I merely didn't do it, and I didn't give the matter a lot of thought.

Timmy planned on returning to Lenox at the end of the workday. So, while Kate prepared the just-departed Grishams' room for its next guests – she could no longer afford the cleaning service she had used for years – I sat on the side porch next to Arthur and read *Master Thieves,* the Stephen

Kurkjian investigation into the Gardner heist that Timmy had read and summarized a few days earlier.

Kurkjian's conclusion that the robbery was done by mobster Bobby Donati and an accomplice was not an opinion shared by the FBI. Donati died in Boston gang warfare a year and a half after the theft, so nobody was going to be able to ask him if he did it, and if so, what had become of the stolen art? The one thing that everybody with an informed opinion agreed on was, local mid- and low-level mobsters – Donati or others – were responsible for the outrage. Remo Chicarelli's name never came up, however, and neither did Monmouth Khachaturian's. Nor did Bucky Costello's name or Fess Tetlow's.

A Kurkjian theory on the thieves' motives made sense for Donati, though not for Khachaturian or Bucky and Fess. Donati had heard of stolen art being used to gain the early release of a fellow mobster. The author believed Donati had that kind of scheme in mind for getting his mob pal Vinnie Ferrara out of prison. The Rembrandts and the other Gardner treasures would be exchanged for Ferrara's freedom. In that explanation, the organizer of the art theft was a humanitarian of a certain perverse type, while Khachaturian, Bucky, and Fess were merely greedy.

I had just finished reading when Kate came outside and said she'd had a call from Special Agent Trout. He told her the FBI planned on locating and interviewing Bucky later in the day – Trout hinted but did not say directly that a warrant had been obtained to search Bucky's home – and the agent asked if Kate would be willing to participate in a Zoom call with other FBI staff intent on learning more about Bucky's personal history and possible current state of mind. She said sure, and the Zoom was set up for 2 p.m.

We had peanut butter and jelly sandwiches for lunch – Timmy wasn't there to take us down to Church Street with his MasterCard – and after some fiddling around with her phone, Kate joined the Zoom call just after two. She said I could sit nearby and jump in if it seemed that might be helpful.

After recounting for an expanded audience the tale of her aunt's deathbed confession and how the cow painting had been vandalized and its alleged hidden treasures spirited away, Kate was asked by Special Agent Trout to talk about her cousin's personal history. She rattled on for a good five minutes. She told about his "troubled youth," including a certain amount of property theft, and of course sucking the nitrous oxide out of the Reddi-Wip cans at Price Chopper. That last part generated several *ohs* and *ahs,* as well as chortles, the FBI apparently never having heard tell of that particular crime.

Kate went on about how Bucky and his mother loved each other unconditionally, and how he seemed to settle down and start behaving himself after he hooked up in his twenties with his beloved Red Sox.

Trout asked her about Bucky's more serious run-ins with the law such as the two assault convictions. "Does your cousin own or carry a firearm?" was an early question on this topic. Kate said she didn't know if he had a gun but she doubted it.

I mouthed *baseball bat,* and she told the FBI Zoom audience that Bucky had a favorite Ted Williams baseball bat, and it was her understanding that Bucky had been known to hit people with it, when provoked.

"Provoked in what way?" a male voice asked.

"When someone insults his mother. Or when someone does something bad to his baseball cards. Tries to steal them or whatever."

I could make out murmurs in the FBI office. I suspected Kate was debating whether or not to mention the baseball bat attack on Sean Cunard. It was likely going to come out soon that it was Cunard who snatched the Gardner art from behind the cow painting and that Bucky then forcibly grabbed the art from Sean. She told me after the Zoom session that she felt a shred of sympathy for Cunard, and if he was going to be put through the wringer by the feds, she figured she would let Bucky be the one who fingered the

Lenox businessman.

Finally, Special Agent Trout asked Kate if she might help the FBI retrieve the Gardner paintings from Bucky by personally urging his cooperation, if it came to that.

She thought for a moment. Then she said, "Of course I would. Conditionally."

CHAPTER 45

THE RED SOX HAD FIVE more days of home games before travelling to Oakland for a series there. The federal agents who now had Bucky under surveillance, we learned later, observed him at work, tending the infield, battening down the bases, resupplying the dugouts with water and energy drinks. The feds obtained Sox senior management's permission to hang around the park incognito, but a number of Fenway workers wondered aloud who these well-dressed fellows they'd never seen before were. It's possible that those conversations – if he overheard them – set off Bucky's suspicions, and they set in motion the preposterous series of events that soon ensued.

Kate and I only learned about the Fenway surveillance part of the scenario later. Back in Lenox, all we knew was that Agent Trout and his fellow officers planned on approaching Bucky at some point soon and questioning him. And probably producing a warrant to search his home, car, and, we supposed, his locker at Fenway Park.

Timmy arrived back from Albany after six and said he was taking two more days of leave. He told Kate and me that Assemblyman Lipschitz was among those who were busy trying to maneuver Andrew Cuomo into resigning, but neither he nor anybody else was having any luck. The governor claimed close-in physical greetings were a Borough of Queens cultural thing that was okay if no tongue was involved. Hands were also all right in most cases.

Before we headed downtown for dinner on Church Street – gainfully employed Timmy invited us – Kate brought him up to date on her Zoom call with the FBI.

"And Agent Trout asked me," she said, finishing up her report, "if I would be willing to help persuade Bucky to cooperate and turn over the Gardner paintings to the authorities, and I said of course I would. On one condition."

A droll look from Timmy. "I'll bet I can get that one on the first guess."

"On the condition that I get some credit toward receiving the museum's reward of ten million dollars."

"Credit? You mean like karmic merit? Or Delta air miles? I'm not sure if it's going to work like that."

Seated across the kitchen table from Timmy and me, Kate was sounding newly sure of herself. "It's not just any assistance I can provide at this point. I was the first person to notify the police of Aunt Mary's confession and the theft from behind the cow painting. If I'm not first in line to collect the reward, then who the hell is?" Her jaw was set and her eyes were luminous.

Timmy is a kind person but also a realist. "Well, it was Father Thigpen who notified the FBI. And they're the ones who took the report seriously. Not the Lenox cops – as you yourself have pointed out on any number of occasions."

She snickered. "What's a Catholic priest going to do with ten million dollars? Especially this one. Buy his boyfriend some Louis Vuitton luggage to take on their trips to visit Marla Jo Vernon?"

"Varla Jean Merman," Timmy gently corrected her. "Supposedly the illegitimate daughter of Ernest Borgnine and Ethel Merman. Not that that makes any sense."

"But fair's fair," Kate went on, undeterred. "Anyway, Agent Trout said he was sure the bureau would go out of its way to show its appreciation for any assistance I might render."

"Yes, I'm sure they will gladly do just that – express their appreciation."

Not wanting Kate to go all the way over the edge with a hope that sounded risky to me, I said, "If they get hold of Bucky and he won't admit to anything, why do you think you'd have all that much influence over him? You two were never close. If he just clams up, what could you do? For that matter, what could anybody do? The one person with actual evidence of Bucky's role in the Gardner theft is Sean Cunard. And there's not much he can really say without incriminating himself. What we might end up with here is a kind of conspiracy of silence between Sean and Bucky, with the Gardner paintings nowhere to be seen. We still don't know what Bucky has actually done with the masterpieces. He could just proclaim his innocence and say he has no idea where the art treasures are, and that might be that."

Kate gave me a sour look.

Timmy put one on, too. "And the FBI would call a press conference and announce that agents had been talking to someone they would call a *person of interest,* but they still had been unable to lay their hands on the long missing great art."

"I'm pretty sure," Kate said, "that I would know what to say to Bucky that would bring him around. I only just need the opportunity to do it."

"You might get that chance," I had to agree. "It's hard to imagine the cousin you have described to me over the past five days sitting down with Special Agents Trout and Brisbane and admitting to anything at all. I can see him telling them that there's a chance of showers and he might have to roll out the tarps during that night's game. And if anybody interfered with his doing that extremely important job, the guilty party, federal agent or not, would bring down on himself the wrath of the people of Boston."

Kate insisted again that she thought she knew a line of argument that could bring Bucky around. I didn't challenge her very forcefully, because it was the same argument I had thought I might employ back when I imagined that I might be the one to track Bucky down and finally meet the despicable museum robber face to face.

This back and forth went on a little longer, and then Kate's phone rang. It was Special Agent Trout informing her that after an afternoon game at Fenway Park, Bucky had been followed to his home in Belmont. When agents knocked on his door and announced that they were the FBI and wished to speak with him, Bucky fled down a fire escape and managed to elude the men positioned at the front and rear doors to his apartment block.

And now, Agent Trout told Kate, Bucky was on the run.

CHAPTER 46

THE AGENTS WHO SHOWED UP at Bucky's apartment with a warrant found out he'd escaped out a window when Bucky's girlfriend Janice opened the door a few minutes later and told them, "He went that way! And he took his goddamn bat, the asshole!"

Janice was irked because she was getting ready to go start her shift at Friendly's, and now she was going to have to talk to these pushy feds for who knew how long, and she was probably going to miss her bus.

Agent Trout also told Kate that Janice believed Bucky blamed his cousin in Lenox for siccing the authorities on him and there was a possibility Bucky might head for Lenox carrying his bat with revenge in mind. Kate told Timmy and me she'd like to explain to Janice that it was Father Thigpen, not her, who went to the FBI. And explain it to Bucky, too – he had no way of knowing that he'd been nailed by the priest who had administered the church's last rites for his all-but-sainted mother.

Bucky's flight served one very useful purpose. It confirmed to the FBI agents that they were actually on the right track this time with the Gardner heist investigation. The big questions now were, where was Bucky, and where were the Rembrandts?

Bucky usually parked his car with all the Red Sox

paraphernalia on it behind the apartment block he and Janice lived in. Janice – still ticked off over the likelihood she'd miss her bus – told the feds to check for the car. It was still there, they found, so how was Bucky going to get around? On foot? On the bus Janice was afraid of missing?

Agent Trout asked Kate if she wished to have protection in case an angry Bucky showed up in Lenox. She said no, she had friends with her, and she thought one of them had a gun. That was me. And I did have a gun – back at the house in Albany. Should I drive home and retrieve it? The drive was an hour over and an hour back, so I guessed I had time. But there was no reason to believe Bucky was carrying a firearm, so I chose not to go get mine. I did consider seeking out a sporting goods store and purchasing a baseball bat. Kate said she had two lesbian friends in nearby Williamsville who had several bats, and Kate was sure we could borrow one.

Bringing Timmy and me further up to date, Kate said, "Agent Trout told me they searched Bucky's apartment and there was no sign of the Gardner art there. There was nothing in his car, either. It sounds as if they are pretty worried about what might have become of the paintings. And God knows, I am, too."

We were sitting on Kate's porch along with Arthur, who seemed bored nearly to tears by all the agitated palaver. He all but had his paws over his ears. It was still light at 7:40, and I realized that it was the day of the summer solstice, sometimes called *the longest day of the year* even though it had only 24 hours in it, not 25 or 26. The sky over Undermountain Road was creamy and still, and in no way resembling Rembrandt's stormy sky over the Sea of Galilee. That was a sky we all hoped to lay eyes on again soon, although we were beginning to wonder about that.

I said, "It's possible Bucky did find a fence and that's where the paintings are now. In Woburn or wherever he's been turning up since he got back in the Boston area from Lenox."

"Just so he didn't burn them or toss them in Boston Harbor," Timmy said. "You know, destroy the evidence."

Kate winced. "Let's not even think about that. I can't really imagine he'd do something that reckless and cruel. He'd know it would be something Aunt Mary would disapprove of, and that would be an insurmountable obstacle in Bucky's mind."

"Bucky is such a Red Sox nut," Timmy said, "that maybe he did something like hide the paintings at Fenway so the Sox could collect the reward. The art might soon turn up in Bucky's locker or somewhere else at the park."

"The pitcher's bull pen," Kate speculated.

"A French finial was also among the items taken in the heist," I reminded them. "Maybe it's already atop the flagpole at the stadium. Somebody should check."

Kate nodded knowingly. "That would be just like Bucky."

"Wasn't there also an old Chinese urn?" Timmy asked. "A ceremonial object? Somebody at Fenway could be eating wonton soup out of it as we speak."

Mention of soup reminded us that Timmy was going to take us out for a nice meal. We were getting ready to head out when Kate's phone rang. It was Agent Trout again. He wanted to know if somehow Bucky had contacted Kate – she said he hadn't – and to make sure Kate continued to feel safe and secure – which she said she did.

Then Agent Trout told Kate something Janice Nestor had told the FBI agents after she missed her bus and was about to be late for work. Janice said Bucky had admitted to her that he might be in trouble with the law. But, he assured his girlfriend, she shouldn't worry because he would soon have something in his possession that he could use for bargaining his way out of any possible charges.

Kate relayed this exchange to Timmy and me. And she said, "He'll have something in his possession *soon*? What's that supposed to mean?"

CHAPTER 47

WE HAD DINNER AT A sidewalk table at the restaurant across the street from Sean Cunard's gallery. Sean's place was still closed, with yellow police tape making a big X on the front door. The inside of the gallery was dark, and nobody had fed the ballerinas in the window.

Timmy insisted we treat ourselves to anything we felt like eating. We did order some tasty dishes – scallops, lamb chops, paella – but the mood when the food arrived was hardly celebratory. Kate and Timmy had wine: I drank beer.

Midway in the meal, my phone signaled that a text had landed. It was who I suspected it might be.

"It's Laurel Peaseley again," I told my companions. "She wants to know if I'm *out of range.* Or if something has happened rendering me *incommunicado.*"

Timmy said, "I'm surprised she didn't ask, *Cat got your tongue, Donnie?*"

"Cell service in Lenox is spotty," Kate noted. "There's your excuse."

"I've noticed," Timmy said, "there are no cell towers in town."

"Everybody wants better service, but nobody wants any towers."

"Not unless," Timmy said, "they're made of wood."

Kate was enjoying her lamb chops, a big step up from a

PBJ. She looked over at me scarfing up my paella. "So I guess, Donald, you'll have to respond to Strathmore pretty soon. I mean, sign the contract. You haven't changed your mind, have you?"

"No. Why would I? Other than the fact that I've been on my own for so many years it's unlikely I'll last long in an organization that talks like Kayleigh McEnany and probably operates like Mohammed bin Salman. I like to think of myself as adaptable. For instance, Timmy and I once spent a week trekking among the hill tribes of Upper Burma eating bugs and drinking a lot of rice wine home brew in order to kill the bacteria. I managed that with no sweat. But adapting to corporate culture is – well, I think you know what I mean. Dear God."

"Maybe," Kate said, "the pandemic will peter out. And your own detective business will pick up again. There are lots of signs the economy is coming back. Criminality will pick up, too. And clients will be in a position again to pay you to do something about it."

I said it could be. "But everything is so uncertain at this point. It does make sense to sign on with Strathmore. I mean, really – where *did* all those bricks in Utica go? And there's bound to be some stuff come up that's actually interesting. And if it didn't work out, what's the worst that could happen? Either I'd quit or they'd fire me. I can't imagine some Jason Bourne situation where they were chasing me around the world trying to do away with me."

"And there's still at least a slim chance Kate can snatch some of the Gardner millions," Timmy said, "and that will solve everybody's financial problems instantaneously."

That got no response. None of us really believed it.

Kate ceased gnawing some lamb remnants off a bone and set the morsel-bearing object down. "I totally don't get Janice saying Bucky would *soon* be in possession of something that will get him off the hook with law enforcement. If he has the Gardner paintings – or just knows where they are – shouldn't *that* be his bargaining chip?"

"Maybe," Timmy said, "I don't know – what? Maybe he mailed the paintings to himself or something. UPS?"

"Or he gave them to somebody for safe-keeping. But if so, who?"

"And now he'll retrieve them and hand them over to the FBI and be hailed in the art world as a savior."

I said, "That could happen. There is the statute of limitations on the theft itself. And the museum might just be so grateful to have its art back that they won't press for any legal action. I can't imagine them forking the ten million over to Bucky, though. These are strange times, I know. But not quite that strange."

Kate's phone rang. She looked at the caller ID and said, "FBI."

A courteous person, Kate placed her napkin on the table, excused herself, and walked ten feet down Church Street, away from our fellow diners.

We could see her mostly listening to presumably Agent Trout but from time to time remarking calmly.

She came back after a few minutes and sat down. "Bucky is on the move. He borrowed a car from a friend who didn't know Bucky was being pursued by the law. He is apparently moving, but with his phone off no one knows where he's going. Agent Trout asked that we keep our eyes out for Bucky showing up around Lenox. I said we would. I asked Trout if he thought Bucky might be heading somewhere to retrieve the Gardner art and use that for making a deal with the authorities."

Timmy asked, "And what did he say?"

"Agent Trout said he hadn't the faintest idea what Bucky was up to, but he felt confident the whole world would know quite soon."

It did.

CHAPTER 48

TIMMY AND I WERE FILLING our coffee mugs in Kate's kitchen early the next morning when we heard her scream.

She had just carried her own coffee into the living room and turned on the TV. She had told us she was going to check out New England Cable News to see if there was anything about Bucky on the lam from the FBI.

"Oh God, oh God," Kate was moaning when we raced in to see what was happening.

A big banner at the bottom of the NECN screen was flashing *BREAKING NEWS BREAKING NEWS BREAKING NEWS!*

The goggle-eyed news anchor was announcing, "Police in Woburn have confirmed an overnight break-in at the Life-Beyond Cryogenics Center on Pillsbury Road. One item was stolen from the facility, which houses the remains of deceased persons who have been frozen by their families with the hope that one day science will be in a position to bring these loved ones back to life. The item stolen from the LBCC is reported to be – incredible as this may sound – the actual *head* of Boston Red Sox great Ted Williams. NECN is attempting to obtain further information on this macabre story, so stay tuned. Williams led the American League in hitting from...."

"*Item*," Timmy said. "Cable news called what Bucky stole an *item*."

I stood staring at the TV. "The news writers must be

beside themselves. Their vocabularies aren't ready for this. Nobody's is."

Kate bleated out, "And of course it was Bucky! This must have been the first thing that popped into his head when he was looking for something to trade for getting the law off his case. For chrissakes, I am so grateful Aunt Mary is not alive to have to process this!"

"So, where's the Gardner art?" Timmy all but shouted. "If he could do a thing like this, who knows what he might have done with the paintings!"

Kate's phone rang and she picked it up. "Yes, I know, I know," she told the caller. "We just saw it on the news. Of *course* it was my cousin! It sounds just like him. It's exactly the type of thing he did when he was fourteen, and now he's at it again."

She listened for another minute, and said, "Naturally I'll do anything I can to help, but I can't imagine what that might be. Bucky has gone all the way around the bend, and the only person who might have had any influence over him at all is underground in Lee Catholic Cemetery. At this point, all I can really say to you, Mr. Trout, is good luck!"

There was another brief exchange and then Kate rang off. "They figured right away it was Bucky. At least they know the car he's driving, and the police are now on the lookout. He is *not* going to get away with this!"

"Yes, your cousin may have overreached this time," Timmy said. "The evidence is only circumstantial that it was Bucky, but I somehow doubt it was a student prank and the place to look for Ted Williams's head is an MIT dorm."

We sat down and gawked at the TV again. NECN had a crawl at the bottom of the screen saying *TED WILLIAMS HEAD MISSING – POLICE SAY PERSON OF INTEREST SOUGHT.* Above the crawl the screen was showing highlights from the Splendid Splinter's career.

Understanding that Bucky's terrible caper would be news worldwide, we switched to CNN, where similar coverage was underway. *BASEBALL GREAT'S HEAD TAKEN – HELD*

HOSTAGE? – FAMILY BEGS FOR RETURN. The anchor was interviewing a Boston *Globe* reporter, who said officials at the cryonics facility were urging the thief to keep the head in a cooler with freezer packs and not let it thaw out under any circumstances.

Timmy said he guessed Bucky would have been smart enough to think of that. "It does raise an interesting question. If anything goes awry with the so-called *item*, could Bucky be charged with murder? I'm guessing Massachusetts state law is not prepared for a situation like this."

CNN switched to a reporter outside Fenway Park, where a crowd had begun to gather. All of them were angry, and some were beside themselves with rage. One elderly man mentioned the death penalty, although it had long since been abolished in Massachusetts. A younger man in a Red Sox cap told the reporter he was sure drugs were involved. Somebody found a way to blame Donald Trump, and another managed to implicate Joe Biden.

The CNN reporter said a number of taverns in the area of the ballpark had received permission by the city to open early to accommodate the crowds clamoring to get inside. As the camera panned around, I noticed people pouring into Jim-bo's tavern, where five days earlier Bucky had bribed a couple of dirty cops with 400 dollars' worth of Sox box seats and found out after years of trying that Miles Tate had become Sean Cunard, and the Lenox purveyor of way-too-skinny ballerinas had almost certainly filched the Gardner masterpieces from behind Bucky's mom's cow painting.

Out of curiosity, I phoned Cunard in his room at Berkshire Medical Center. I wondered if he was aware of what Bucky was up to at the present moment.

"I'm watching it all on TV," Cunard croaked out. "Everybody at the hospital is. The nurse said a lot of patients are very upset, and the staff have to keep passing out blood pressure meds. What I'm wondering, naturally, is why Bucky thought he had to pull an appalling stunt like this? I mean, where the fuck are the Gardner paintings? They were in pretty decent shape when Bucky beat me up and left with the art in a garbage bag. What the hell did the stupid jerk do with that incredible bag of goodies?"

It seemed as if we would all have the answer to that question soon. Wouldn't we?

CHAPTER 49

JUST PAST ELEVEN that morning, the governor of Massachusetts held a press conference. This very blue state had a Republican governor; Kate and Timmy both knew that the generally liberal electorate elected Republican governors to keep an eye on the Democratic crooks in the Legislature. Now, the tall, stony-faced Republican governor of Massachusetts was surrounded on the State House steps by aides, federal and state law enforcement officials, Democratic leaders of the state House and Senate, and by weeping members of the Ted Williams family.

Bucky's name was not mentioned. The governor just talked about "the perpetrator" and pleaded with him to, "for the love of God," return the "human body part" to its rightful place in Woburn or at least to the nearest police station. The governor also reiterated the importance of the perpetrator's using a freezer pack.

Reporters asked many questions, but neither the governor nor the State Police captain at the microphones was prepared to provide much information beyond the time and place of the break-in. Implicit in some questions were criticisms of the Life-Beyond Cryogenics Center's security procedures. It sounded as if the security situation there was similar to that at the Gardner Museum in 1990.

As Timmy, Kate and I watched all this unfold from comfortable seats in Kate's living room, we noted Special Agent Trout among the officials standing near the governor looking anxious. It was unusual for the FBI to appear at a press conference and have nothing to say. We guessed Agent Trout was waiting to see how this all turned out.

As were millions "across the nation and around the world," as CNN put it.

We had all the doors and several windows open – it was another splendid June day in the Berkshires – and we listened for the sound of any car pulling into Kate's driveway. We couldn't think of a reason Bucky might show up back in Lenox, but if Bucky had a second middle name besides Chutzpah, it had to be Unpredictable.

"I do hope he's not planning to come here," Kate said at one point. "I don't know how much space I have in my freezer."

"He'd never make it all the way to Lenox," Timmy said. "The cops are looking for the car he borrowed, and they would nab him on the interstate, wouldn't they?"

"He could take back roads," I said, "and maybe slip by small-town cops during their off-duty hours. He could also have switched cars somehow."

That night's Sox game with Houston had been cancelled, and by mid-afternoon crowds had begun to fill Fenway Park, which the Red Sox management opened up for a prayer vigil starting at 6:30 p.m. NECN reported that Boston merchants were reporting a run on candles and mylar balloons.

Kate checked, and the internet was aflame with conspiracy theories and wild ideas as to who the perpetrator was. Radical Islamists were mentioned repeatedly. Some speculated that the head would be offered back to the cryonics center in return for the release of Dzhokhar Tsarnaev, the imprisoned Boston Marathon bomber. Also accused were Antifa, the Proud Boys, and the Democratic National Committee. Facebook was full of accusations by people who knew of relatives they were sure were involved. Somebody claimed to have information that it was a cadre of unhinged New York

Yankees fans.

Kate read some of this to Timmy and me. She was red-faced with alternating anger and embarrassment. "This is all just such a horrible thing for the Costello family. And the Winklemans, Aunt Mary's family down in Tyringham. A number of the Winklemans were what you'd have to call eccentric. Occasionally it was more than that. Aunt Mary had an aunt, Lucinda Winkleman, who had what the family called *sticky fingers*. Whenever the Federated Church had a tea, they'd appoint at least three people to keep an eye on the silver.

"Around the same time, Clarence Winkleman was the town fence viewer. For several years, he did a good job settling any farm property disputes that arose. By the time he was in his late forties, though, Mr. Winkleman simply spent long hours every day sitting on a camp stool he carried around with him and staring at fences.

"Aunt Mary was very much in that Winkleman family tradition of small misdemeanors and harmless odd habits. And now Bucky has blown the small-town quaintness of it all completely out of the water with his appalling cruel stunt. When this all comes out, the Winklemans won't be merely chuckled at, but despised. And in an example of the worst kind of guilt by association, the Costellos will be, too. I *hate* Bucky for this, and if I get the chance to meet him again face to face, I am not going to reason with him for the FBI. I am going to wring his neck!"

Neither Timmy nor I could think of anything we might say to comfort Kate in any meaningful way. It wasn't much later, though, that Kate suddenly had no time to sit and stew over her family's ruined reputation. She was too busy closing in on the missing Rembrandts.

CHAPTER 50

AGENT TROUT PHONED KATE again just before seven o'clock. We had spent the entire day in front of her living room TV set and were settling in to watch coverage of the prayer vigil at Fenway Park.

When Trout told Kate he was requesting her "urgent immediate assistance," she went to speaker-phone so that Timmy and I would know what was happening.

"I'll help if I can," Kate told him, though she was looking mystified.

"It is not yet publicly known, and I am requesting that you not talk about this to anyone. But your cousin, Walter Costello, phoned our office at six-twenty-seven p.m.," the agent intoned, "and he confessed to both robberies, the Gardner Museum and the cryogenics facility."

"I'm relieved to hear it," Kate stated. "Maybe now we're getting somewhere." She did not add, "After you people chased your own tails fecklessly for thirty-one years."

Sounding uncharacteristically breathless for a federal agent, Trout went on, "Fortunately, for the Williams family – and for Mr. Williams himself – your cousin is willing to return Mr. Williams's head on two conditions."

Timmy and I glanced at each other. Was any of this actually happening?

Kate just said, "Oh, really? What conditions?"

"One is, Walter wants state Attorney General Maura Healey to grant him immunity from prosecution for stealing the head. He told us telephonically from a pay phone at a service plaza on Route 128 that he had only stolen the head in order to strike a deal having to do with the Gardner art. He said he means Mr. Williams no harm."

"I'm surprised Bucky even knows who Maura Healey is. Did he say he was ready to tell you where to find the art?"

"That's where the second condition comes in," the FBI man said. "The second condition is, he wants to meet with you, and *you* have to agree to something. That is, before the matter of the art is resolved."

"You have to be kidding. Agree to what?"

"Your cousin declined to say what it was he wanted you to do. But whatever it is, Mrs. Webster, we are asking you kindly to please seriously consider doing it. Provided, of course, it's nothing illegal. We'd have to check with DC Headquarters, as to that."

"What about the head? And the first condition? Immunity from prosecution for stealing Ted Williams's head. What does Maura Healey have to say about that? I mean, that's kind of hilarious."

"Hilarious?"

"I mean weird. Weird is all I mean."

"The Bureau's general counsel is in contact with the Massachusetts attorney general at this moment. So, are you going to cooperate? I – I urge you to do so. So much that's important to the people of Boston – and to sports enthusiasts around the world – hinges on your decision. I hear your television on in the background, so I don't think I need to spell out any more clearly how much we are counting on you and how critically important this is."

"I hear you, Mr. Trout. I get the picture."

"And it's vital that all this is resolved tonight. I mean, ASAP. Let me put it this way, Mrs. Webster. Have you ever accidentally left a rump roast out on the kitchen counter overnight?"

I could make out Timmy muttering, "That's way too vivid."

Kate said into the phone, "So, is Bucky going to call me, or what? The last I knew, his phone was turned off."

"He insists on meeting you in person. In the Boston area at a location he will notify us of at one a.m."

"One a.m.? Normally I'm asleep at that hour. God. But – okay, sure. My friends that you met the other day, Timothy Callahan and Donald Strachey, can drive me. I've had a couple of glasses of wine and I'm not quite up to getting all the way to the end of the pike on my own."

Kate glanced over at us and we nodded yes.

"There's no need for that, Mrs. Webster. Agent Brisbane and I will pick you up, and your friends may accompany you if you feel you need support."

"Oh, I do."

"We are actually on the pike now," Trout said, "with a State Police escort. Our Lenox ETA is approximately eleven-oh-two."

"Sure, see you then," Kate said, and then sat there looking at Timmy and me and shaking her head.

At exactly 11:02, what sounded like a sizeable fleet of vehicles pulled into Kate's driveway. Doors slammed, and lights began flashing this way and that way. We went out on the porch to greet the throng, which must have caused porch lights to go on up and down Undermountain Road.

Timmy said, "It's like in *The Third Man* when they were chasing Harry Lime through the sewers of Vienna."

Special agents Trout and Brisbane, clad in their Hoover-era business suits, were accompanied by a small militia of mostly men and a few women in sportier all-black outfits that said *FBI* in big letters on the front and back. Several were wielding wands of some sort.

At some point, a Lenox police cruiser had met the armada from Boston and accompanied it into the driveway. Once we were loaded into a big SUV and were on the road, Kate asked Trout, "How much have the Lenox cops been told as to what this is all about?"

"Only that you have information that will help the Bureau recover Mr. Williams's body part."

Kate laughed once. "Oh, swell."

CHAPTER 51

THE BELMONT FRIENDLY'S was closed up and dark at one-twenty a.m. There was just one car in the parking lot. Agent Trout recognized the vehicle, an aged Ford Escort, as the one Bucky had borrowed from a friend the day before and had not returned.

When he phoned Trout at one, Bucky had insisted that he would speak only to Kate, a family member. She said she was frightened and asked that a future family member, her fiancé – that was going to be me – accompany her, and Bucky said, okay, just so he's not a cop. He also insisted on no recording devices. The FBI agents wanted to wire both of us up, but Kate said no, that wasn't the deal that had been made with her cousin.

The convoy of black SUVs positioned themselves around the various entrances and exits to the restaurant parking lot. Kate, Timmy and I were in the lead vehicle, which parked about 20 yards from Bucky's borrowed car.

The air was cool but clear, with a bright white half moon illuminating the unfolding drama.

"Hey, Kate, this is all your fault, goddamn it," Bucky said, as we walked up to him. He was leaning against the car wearing his Sox cap. He had aged from the photos I'd seen of him, and the years of ball games and beer were showing on his tired face and a midsection close to full bloom. He was not holding anything – a garbage bag, a gym bag, a baseball bat, or anything else.

"No, it's your fault, Bucky. I didn't steal the Rembrandts, and I didn't steal Ted Williams's head. You did. So now, what are you going to do to make things right? The way your mother would want you to do. I mean, what's the deal here?"

"Okay, Kate. Just stop bugging me about Mom, okay? You always do that, and I am sick and tired. So please just *lay off!*" Looking at me, he said, "You marrying my uppity cousin? Well, good luck with that."

I kept my mouth shut and Kate ignored the taunt. "Why should I not bug you about your mom? She was my aunt, and I loved Aunt Mary. I loved her for doing everything in her power to make the world a better place for all its inhabitants to live and breathe in. For preserving our water resources and our flowers, too. She left Berkshire County a cleaner, greener, even lovelier place then it was when she was born. And do you know what else she wanted to protect and keep from harm?"

"Yeah, those freakin' paintings from the freakin' Gardner Museum."

"I mean you, Bucky. Your mom wanted more than anything for you to live and be well and stay the hell out of the goddamn clink. Now I don't know how you are going to do that, having really fucked up royally this time around."

Bucky smirked. "Maura Healey is going to grant me impunity. Those guys who drove you here told me that, and somebody at Fenway told me it's illegal for the FBI to lie to people."

"How do you even know who Maura Healey is?"

"Those FBI guys told me. I asked who was in charge of shit like this, and they said this chick Maura. Anyway, Kate, I guess now *I* have all these dudes over a great big barrel, don't I?"

I piped up and said, "Bucky, you just said a mouthful."

"A mouthful of what?"

"Of truer words were never spoken. "That you've got us *all* over a barrel."

"So, Bucky," Kate said, "you decided to drag *me* into this for some weird reason. What's that about, cousin?"

Bucky looked down. "I really am sorry for some of the things I did. I mean it."

"You should be."

"And I know I shouldn't have grabbed Mr. Williams's head. Even though he told me to go suck a lemon that one time, I did something very disrespectful."

"His family members are begging you to return it."

"I know. And I will. I just needed it to get you over here to make one promise."

In the moonlight, I could make out Kate's look of deep puzzlement. "Me? Why me?"

His pudgy face tightened with pain. "So here's the deal, cousin. I promise to return Mr. Williams's head if you promise not to tell everybody in Lenox that Mom was a big crook."

"Oh, Bucky."

"And say that, like, she didn't know the Gardner paintings were behind the cows all those years. Just say she just found out. Just say I confessed that to her last week when I popped it at Mount Mercy, and then she told you."

"Oh, dear."

"People trust you, Kate. That's one reason I never liked you very much. I'm sorry to say stuff like that, like I'm some asshole, but I guess I have to tell the truth this time."

"Never too late."

"So, will you do that?"

She hesitated no more than a second. "Sure."

"You promise to keep Mom totally out of this shit that I admit I got myself into up to my eyeballs."

"I promise."

"And you'll make her do it, right?" He was talking to me.

"You bet I will."

"Okay. Then here's the deal. You can tell those FBI dudes over there that Mr. Williams's head is inside."

"Inside what?"

"Inside Friendly's. This is where Janice works. They know

me here. I came by early this morning and said Janice asked me to leave a barbecued chicken in their walk-in freezer and she would pick it up tomorrow – she's off today. The assistant manager said okay. I was afraid he might think it was a bomb and check the gym bag it was in, but he didn't. I think he saw it was a Sox bag, so it had to be okay."

"Oh. Well. Good. Bucky, you're doing the right thing. And think of how grateful all the Sox fans will be. Especially the older ones who still remember when."

"I still hope," Bucky said sadly, "that I will live long enough to see Mr. Williams brought back to life. Maybe I'll be an old man, and I'll meet him, and I'll say, hey, Mr. Williams, you probably don't remember me. But when I was a kid, you told me to go suck a lemon. And when I was fifty-five and you were in a freezer bag in Woburn I took your head for a little spin down to Belmont. Maybe he'll think it's kind of funny."

"I hope it works out that way. For both of you."

"Yeah, if my freakin' luck changes for the better."

"There is another thing, Bucky."

"I know."

"The Gardner Museum art. Is it – okay?"

"Oh, sure."

"Can it be returned to the museum?"

"I think so."

"So where is it?"

Bucky looked at me and said, "I can only tell that to somebody who is presently in the family. Donald, you have to go over there with the feds for just a minute. By the way, congratulations. When's the wedding? Maybe I'll come."

I smiled and said, "No date set yet," and walked away toward the FBI vehicle containing Agents Trout and Brisbane.

As he stepped out of the car, Trout asked urgently, "So where is Mr. Williams's head?"

"I'll tell you shortly. I want to watch this."

I saw Bucky lean in toward Kate and speak to her. And then, like Barbara Stanwyck in a forties screwball comedy doing a take, she slapped her forehead with the palm of her hand and all but fell over.

Soon, Kate strode over to the FBI agents, both of them standing outside the SUV now, and she told them where the Ted Williams head was, it being safe in cold storage. Somebody yelled, "Get an axe!"

Then we waited for her to tell us where the Gardner Museum's long lost great art was located at the present moment. Kate said to the agents, "I'll tell you tomorrow first thing. Before I do, I have to talk to a priest."

CHAPTER 52

FATHER THIGPEN, WHEN KATE spoke to him in the morning, agreed to say – if asked – that Mary Costello had told him she had only recently been informed that the Gardner master-pieces were hidden behind her cow painting. Not that she had been harboring them there for 31 years. The priest told Kate this lie was another Augustinian-style example of a small evil for a greater good. That is, getting Bucky to announce where the stolen art had been most recently tucked away.

In the Lee Catholic Cemetery, Mary Costello was disin-terred on a gorgeous late June morning similar to the one during which she – and the Gardner masterpieces – had been lowered into the ground on the day of her funeral. During his private final visit to the McGonigal Funeral Home, Bucky had nestled the art in its garbage bag snugly beneath his moth-er's remains for safe keeping by her art-loving spirit for all eternity. And then when Terry McGonigal entered the room, Bucky recited a prayer he remembered from childhood while the funeral director closed the coffin lid for what was to be the last time.

Representatives of the Isabella Stewart Gardner Muse-um were there for the raising of the coffin. They had brought with them a cadre of art restorers and preservationists along with an armored truck. They carried the art into the truck, examined it, and declared it to be in not too bad a shape, all things considered. Plans were made to get the paintings and drawings back on display in the museum within a few months, under the protection of the institution's much improved security system.

With Bucky's help, the other two items taken in the original heist were also returned. Soon after the robbery, Bucky had left the French antique finial outside the Lenox Fire Department, where members didn't recognize it and guessed it was a local resident's donation. When asked to do so by the Gardner's board of directors, the department happily took the object down from their flagpole and gave it back to the museum. The ancient Chinese ceremonial urn was actually out in the open in Bucky's apartment. Janice had been keeping the pennies from her Friendly's tips in it, but she said she would turn it over and place her pennies in a sock – which she would then use for hitting Bucky over the head.

Otherwise, Janice stuck with Bucky throughout the entire post-art-recovery settling of accounts. She told a reporter that the Ted Williams escapade was "typical."

Bucky had many legal problems to contend with, but he obtained an excellent Boston lawyer who signed on with the world's most notorious art/human head thief in return for the vast publicity. Bucky was right, of course, about the Gardner heist "statue of limitations." Prosecution was no longer legally possible. The Ted Williams head episode, however, was more problematical. The swift return of the body part was a legal plus, and also a defense fund was set up by some Yankees fans. Bucky had been a loyal and hard-working groundskeeper for over 30 years, so the Sox kept him on while his legal problems were being sorted out.

Sean Cunard had the law breathing down his neck on a number of fronts. He also obtained a slick lawyer, "Fast Eddie" Pontefiasca, of Pittsfield, and managed to stay out of jail. Kate told us later that she heard Cunard had relocated to Sedona, Arizona, where he was dealing in crystals and doing past-life consultations – he claimed to have had experience – with well-heeled tourists from California.

Marcel Descantienne's niece moved to Lenox from France and ran the former Cunard Gallery. The undernourished ballerina business continued to boom.

Kate Webster did not collect the Gardner Museum's ten-million-dollar reward. Her – and my – involvement in the art's recovery was deemed by the shmucks who ran the place as "too indirect." They did give us a one-year free membership to the museum.

Instead, since it was Mary Costello who "discovered the location" of the missing art in her living room, and it was her confession to Father Thigpen that led ultimately to its recovery, Mrs. Costello was declared the rightful recipient of the reward. Of course, she was dead, and Bucky was her heir, and the museum certainly wasn't going to give it to *him.*

Some people in Lenox wondered how Mrs. Costello could have discovered the paintings in her living room just before her death, since she had been bedridden at Mount Mercy for many months prior to her passing. But the consensus around town was, she was such a sweetheart and let's not think about that.

There was some discussion at the museum, the Boston *Globe* reported, of donating the ten million to a favorite charity of Mary Costello's. But nobody was sure what that charity might be – the Lenox Garden Club wouldn't know what to do with such a huge sum – so the museum just decided to keep the money.

Kate ended up okay. Though she never got the reward, press coverage of the known events led to good things. Kate was offered the job of running one of the ugly new chain hotels on the Pittsfield-Lenox Road – the one that looked like a gigantic version of Norman Bates's house in *Psycho* – and her salary would have added up to a nice chunk of change. But she had a better idea and said no thanks. Instead, she redecorated her B&B on Undermountain Road with posters from the Gardner Museum and named her inn Rembrandt House. Business has been excellent.

I didn't go to work for Strathmore investigations. I took

too long to respond to their job offer and they withdrew it. I heard later that senior management there were saying it had been a close call, that they had almost hired me, but later on it had become clear that I was "unstable."

Word did get around that I had been somehow involved in recovery of the Gardner Museum treasures, and I landed several lucrative jobs recovering art stolen from rich collectors. One of those jobs was in Asuncion the winter after the Gardner Museum adventure. I did not succeed at getting an elderly brewery owner's Picasso back. But Timmy went along with me, and it was great getting out of Albany and heading off to summery Paraguay in the month of January.

In February, we drove over to Lenox for a one-night Valentine's Day visit with Kate. We had a small room with a double bed in the back of the house, as all her more commodious rooms were occupied by skiers, snow-shoers, and tourists from the Netherlands who had heard about the inn for Rembrandt lovers in New England.

Sitting by the fire in Kate's living room, with Arthur staring at the floor nearby, we reminisced about our amazing Gardner Museum art treasure adventure.

"We didn't get rich," Kate said, "but our karmic merit situation couldn't be better. Not that my present-life existence is too shabby. I'm pretty much booked up for the next six months. Everybody loves Rembrandt, and I am not at all too proud to exploit my tenuous connection to that great, life-giving, life-loving, humor-filled man. Also, it doesn't hurt to have Samantha and Travis back from Fiji to help me change the sheets."

"The chain hotels out on the highway," Timmy said, "are probably envious. They'll start changing their names to things like Titian House."

Kate laughed. "Or Francis Bacon."

I told Kate I was so glad she had landed on her feet financially. "But I still think it's unfair that those cheap board members at the museum didn't at least toss you a shekel or two. Father Thigpen made the initial report to the FBI, but it was you who finessed everything in the end by getting Bucky to tell the world the lost art was underground in the Lee Catholic Cemetery."

"How true, how true," Kate said, waving her wine glass. "And the funny thing is, the deal Bucky offered me for returning the art treasures, as well as Ted Williams's head – his confession in return for our protecting his mother's good name – was a variation on the arrangement we'd been planning to offer him if we had tracked him down on our own."

"That's a nice way of putting it, Kate. *Variation.* If I had caught up with him, I was prepared to tell him he either returned the Gardner art or I was going to blacken his mother's name up and down Berkshire County. Tell an *Eagle* reporter that Mary Costello was the Ma Barker of Lenox. That she got the Rembrandts out from behind her cow painting on weekends, laid them out on her kitchen table, and cackled."

"That was my plan, too," Kate said. "Say to him if he didn't return the paintings, I'd tell the Garden Club members and her St. Agnes Sodality group that his mom was one of the original robbers of the museum. That I'd even seen her cop uniform and her fake mustache in the hall closet on Walker Street."

"That's pretty brutal," Timmy said. "But I guess justifiable in this case. Even though it's not a human life we're talking about here. It's just art."

Kate and I both sat up straighter, and she said, "Let's not even *start* to have *that* conversation."

Even Arthur looked up.

RICHARD STEVENSON

RICHARD STEVENSON is the pseudonym of Richard Lipez, author of 19 books, including the Don Strachey private eye series. A former editorial writer at The Berkshire Eagle, Lipez reviewed mysteries and thrillers for *The Washington Post*. His reporting, reviews, and fiction appeared in *Newsday, The Boston Globe, The Atlantic, Harper's*, and many other publications. Four of the Strachey books have been filmed by HereTV. *Red White Black and Blue*, the twelfth Strachey book, won the Lambda Literary Award for Best Gay Mystery in 2011. The first in a new PI series, *Knock Off the Hat: A Clifford Waterman Mystery*, set in Philadelphia in 1947, was published in 2022 by Amble Press. Lipez grew up and was educated in Pennsylvania and taught in the Peace Corps in Ethiopia. He was married to sculptor and video artist Joe Wheaton and lived in Becket, Massachusetts. Richard Stevenson passed away in March, 2022.

About ReQueered Tales

In the heady days of the late 1960s, when young people in many western countries were in the streets protesting for a new, more inclusive world, some of us were in libraries, coffee shops, communes, retreats, bedrooms and dens plotting something even more startling: literature – highbrow and pulp – for an explicitly gay audience. Specifically, we were craving to see our gay lives – in the closet, in the open, in bars, in dire straits and in love – reflected in mystery stories, sci-fi and mainstream fiction. Hercule Poirot, that engaging effete Belgian creation of Agatha Christie might have been gay ... Sherlock Holmes, to all intents and purposes, was one woman shy of gay ... but where were the genuine gay sleuths, where the reader need not read between the lines?

Beginning with Victor J Banis's "Man from C.A.M.P." pulps in the mid-60s – riotous romps spoofing the craze for James Bond spies – readers were suddenly being offered George Baxt's Pharoah Love, a black gay New York City detective, and a real turning point in Joseph Hansen's gay California insurance investigator, Dave Brandstetter, whose world weary Raymond Chandleresque adventures sold strongly and have never been out of print.

Over the next three decades, gay storytelling grew strongly in niche and mainstream publishing ventures. Even with the huge public crisis – as AIDS descended on the gay community beginning in the early 1980s – gay fiction flourished. Stonewall Inn, Alyson Publications, and others nurtured authors and readers ... until mainstream success seemed to come to a halt. While Lambda Literary Foundation had started to recognize work in annual awards about 1990, mainstream publishers began to have cold feet. And then, with the rise of e-books in the new millennium which enabled a new self-publishing industry ... there was both an avalanche of new talent coming to market and burying of print authors who did not cross the divide.

The result?

Perhaps forty years of gay fiction – and notably gay and lesbian mystery, detective and suspense fiction – has been teetering on the brink of obscurity. Orphaned works, orphaned authors, many living and some having passed away – with no one to make the case for their creations to be returned to print (and e-print!). General fiction and non-fiction works embracing gay lives, widely celebrated upon original release, also languished as mainstream publishers shifted their focus.

Until now. That is the mission of ReQueered Tales: to keep in circulation this treasure trove of fantastic fiction. In an era of ebooks, everything of value ought to be accessible. For a new generation of readers, these mystery tales, and works of general fiction, are full of insights into the gay world of the 1960s, '70s, '80s and '90s. For those of us who lived through the period, they are a delightful reminder of our youth and reflect some of our own struggles in growing up gay in those heady times.

We are honored, here at ReQueered Tales, to be custodians shepherding back into circulation some of the best gay and lesbian fiction writing and hope to bring many volumes to the public, in modestly priced, accessible editions, world-wide, over the coming years.

So please join us on this adventure of discovery and rediscovery of the rich talents of writers of recent years as the PIs, cops and amateur sleuths battle forces of evil with fierceness, humor and sometimes a pinch of love.

The ReQueered Tales Team

Justene Adamec • Alexander Inglis • Matt Lubbers-Moore

Mysteries from ReQueered Tales

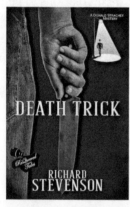

Death Trick
Richard Stevenson

A Don Strachey Mystery, Book 1 – Don Strachey isn't exactly the most sought-after private eye in Albany, New York. In fact, this gay P.I. has gotten to the point of having to write checks to pay his tab at the cheapest lunch counter in town. And he isn't sure that the latest one, for the grand total of two dollars and ninety-three cents, is going to clear.

Surprisingly he's hired to locate Billy Blount, the gay heir to one of Saratoga Springs' upper-crust families. On top of that, Billy, a young and outspoken gay activist, is wanted for the grizzly murder of the man he slept with on his last night in Albany – a man he'd never met before that night.

"Sassy and sexy ... Don Strachey is a private dick who really earns his title." — *Armistead Maupin*

"This murder mystery, recounted with sassiness and wit, is full of true-to-life details about contemporary gay existence. Stevenson uses the yarn to poke fun at straitlaced parents, homophobic cops and greedy gay bar owners ... This is a great lazy-day read – and politically correct, yet!" — *The Advocate*

Written just before the onslaught of AIDS, *Death Trick* is a time capsule of gay life as it existed in smaller towns in America. A foreword for the 2022 edition by Michael Nava (Henry Rios series) is included.

On The Other Hand, Death
Richard Stevenson

A Don Strachey Mystery, Book 2 – When the giant Millpond Company finds its plans for a mega-shopping mall stymied by the refusal of an elderly lesbian couple to sell their home, the ladies are subjected to ugly vandalism and frightening death threats.

The powerful director of Millpond in turn hires Don Strachey, Albany's only gay detective, to protect the ladies, find the culprits, and clear the corporate name. Strachey accepts with misgivings that deepen rapidly as kidnapping, extortion, and murder darken the lives of Albany's gay community.

> "Mystery fans had better grab hold of this and keep an eye out for Richard Stevenson."" — *Bay Area Reporter*

> "The plotting is fast and clever; the gay background works; and the lesbians are engaging characters." — *Publishers Weekly*

Written at the beginning of AIDS activism, *On the Other Hand, Death* is a time capsule of gay life as it existed in smaller towns in America. An author's note is included.

And don't miss ...

Ice Blues: Shocked to discover the body of the grandson of the godfather of Albany's political machine in his car, P.I. Donald Strachey knows he is in for trouble. But when he learns that the murder victim left a $2.5 million legacy with instructions that it be used to destroy that machine, along with a personal letter to Strachey asking for his help, his suspicions are confirmed. Faced with power-brokers at all levels, Albany's only gay P.I. tries to fulfill the dead man's mission-with his own survival at stake.

.

In the Game
Nikki Baker

A Virginia Kelly Mystery, Book 1 – When businesswoman Virginia Kelly meets her old college chum Bev Johnson for drinks late one night, Bev confides that her lover, Kelsey, is seeing another woman. Ginny had picked up that gossip months ago, but she is shocked when the next morning's papers report that Kelsey was found murdered behind the very bar where Ginny and Bev had met. Worried that her friend could be implicated, Ginny decides to track down Kelsey's killer and contacts a lawyer, Susan Coogan. Susan takes an immediate, intense liking to Ginny, complicating Ginny's relationship with her live-in lover. Meanwhile Ginny's inquiries heat up when she learns the Feds suspected Kelsey of embezzling from her employer.

"The auspicious debut of a black writer who brings us a sharp, funny and on-the-mark murder mystery."
— *Northwest Gay & Lesbian Reader*

"An entertaining assortment of female characters makes Baker's debut promising" — *Publishers Weekly*

"It has adventure, romance, and some of the best internal dialogue anywhere." — Megan Casey

Nikki Baker is the first African-American author in the lesbian mystery genre and her protagonist, Virginia Kelly is the first African-American lesbian detective in the genre. Interwoven into the narrative are observations on the intersectionality of being a woman, an African-American, and a lesbian in a "man's" world of finance and life in general.

First published to acclaim in 1991, this new edition features a foreword by the author.

And don't miss ...

The Lavender House Murder: Ginny and Noami in Provincetown

Long Goodbyes: A Christmas return home ends in murder

The Always Anonymous Beast
Lauren Wright Douglas

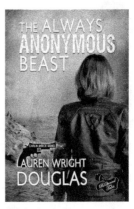

A Caitlin Reece Mystery, Book 1 – Val Frazier, Victoria's star TV anchorwoman, is Caitlin's newest client. She is the victim of a viciously homophobic blackmailer who has discovered her relationship with Tonia Konig. Tonia is a lesbian-feminist professor, an outspoken, passionately committed proponent of nonviolence. She is enraged by her own helplessness, she is outraged by Caitlin's challenge to her most fundamental beliefs, and by Caitlin herself, whom she considers "a thug".

As Caitlin stalks the blackmailer and his accomplices through the byways of the city of Victoria, she uncovers ever darker layers of danger surrounding Tonia. And she struggles against a new and altogether unwanted complication: she is increasingly attracted to the woman who despises her.

"A very accomplished first novel, which is distinguishable by an elegant flair for description and an obvious love of the language." — Karen Axness, *Feminist Bookstore News*

"Douglas' book is snappily written, peppered with wit and literary allusions, and filled with original characters."
— Sherri Paris, *The Women's Review of Books*

Douglas's debut novel in 1987 began a six part series for Caitlin Reece. This new edition includes an introduction by the author and a foreword by legendary Katherine V. Forrest.

And don't miss ...

Ninth Life: Caitlin is hired by a woman code-named Shrew, to pick up a package. Caitlin is sickened to the depths of her being by the contents of the package: a blind and maimed cat, and photographs of animal experimentation. And now Shrew is dead. As a member of the militant animal rights organization Ninth Life, she had infiltrated Living World, a cosmetics company. The other members of Ninth Life suspect she was betrayed by someone within their own ranks and murdered because of what she learned.

A Body to Dye For
Grant Michaels

A Stan Kraychik Mystery, Book 1 – Stan "Vannos" Kraychik isn't your everyday Boston hairdresser. Manager of Snips Salon, which is owned by best bud (and occasional nemesis) Nicole, Stan thought this day was an ordinary one. A delivery van backed into the salon's rear driveway and accidentally spilled gallons of conditioner, leaving Stan and hunky Roger) embracing in a gooey mess trying to staunch the flow, with little success as they slid and slipped with Nicole watching on with rolling eyes. Later Roger is found murdered.

Stan's client, Calvin Redding, who owns the apartment where Roger's body was found, can't explain why the body is dressed in little more than bowties. Enter Lieutenant Branco, dark, muscular, Italian, (straight) of Boston PD Homicide who immediately suspects everyone, especially Stan. In an attempt to clear his name, Stan travels to California, takes up mountain climbing, eavesdropping, spying, schmoozing, and a little bit of schtupping, all in an attempt to find the truth.

Grant Michaels' zany series of adventures starring Stan Kraychik garnered multiple Lambda Literary Awards including a 1991 nomination for Best Gay Men's Mystery. For this new edition, Carl Mesrobian reminisces about his brother Grant in an exclusive foreword, and Neil S. Plakcy provides an introduction of appreciation.

And don't miss ...

Love You to Death: Stan visits a chocolate factory after a patron drops dead at a chi-chi cocktail party

Dead on Your Feet: Stan's new boyfriend, choreographer Rafik, is accused of murder

Mask for a Diva: Stan nabs a gig as wig master to a summer opera festival but the final curtain for one star comes down early

Time to Check Out: Stan takes a holiday to Key West but a dead bodies turns up anyway

Dead as a Doornail: In the midst of renovating his new Boston brownstone, Stan becomes the (unintended?) murder target

Sunday's Child
Edward O. Phillips

A Geoffry Chadwick Misadventure, Book 1 – Lawyer Geoffry Chadwick is 50, Canadian, single, gay and, after a brief struggle with a hustler who tries to shake him down, a murderer. Herein lies the device for this macabre, funny, first novel. Although Geoffry must dispose of the body – which he does by dropping off sections of it around town at night – the trauma of the murder affords him the opportunity to reminisce and ruminate: on the recent termination of his affair with a history teacher; on the not-so-recent deaths of his wife and daughter; on the alcoholism of his mother; on growing old; on being gay. The visit of a nephew and the New Year's festivities only serve to intensify his thoughts. Although Chadwick is abrasively disdainful early on, he is fascinating when he loosens up. Phillips keeps the reader hopping with throwaway quotations from Donne and scatological references and puns.

First published in 1981, and a Books in Canada First Novel nominee, this new edition contains a foreword by Alexander Inglis.

And don't miss …

Buried on Sunday: "One of the problems with weekends in the country" says Geoffry Chadwick's genial host in *Buried on Sunday*, "is that people feel free to drop in unannounced." And sometimes that includes criminals on the lam: forget the hors d'oeuvres, everyone is now hostage. Winner of the coveted Arthur Ellis Best Novel Award from the Crime Writers of Canada.

Sunday Best: Geoffry gets roped into planning a wedding for his niece Jennifer, but the groom has closet issues and a sexy latino chauffeur has a mixed agenda. Then there is widowed Montreal socialite Lois, mother to the groom, who casts her net for Geoffry …

Working on Sunday: Geoffry Chadwick has a stalker. But between avoiding Christmas parties, gift shopping, moving his mother into a senior living facility, handling his recently widowed sister, and dealing with the loss of his long-term boyfriend Patrick, Geoffry Chadwick does not have time for a stalker.

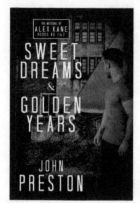

Sweet Dreams / Golden Years
The Missions of Alex Kane
John Preston

The Alex Kane Missions, Books 1 & 2 – Meet Alex Kane. In Vietnam, the only lover he had known had been killed by a homophobic coward. With his physical prowess and the financial backing of his former lover's family Kane's sorrow turned to action, and he is resolved to fight back against anyone, anywhere who dares to challenge the dreams of gay men.

In *Sweet Dreams*, someone was daring to mess with young gay men in Boston. Danny Fortelli, a high school senior and superb gymnast, gets caught up in a drugs-and-prostitution ring exploiting gay youth. Boston's South End had become the epicenter of violence driven by a corrupt elite. Enter Alex Kane to alter their plans forever.

In *Golden Years*, Joe Talbot, long retired and now widowed, dreams of an easier life in a gay retirement community that sounds too good to be true. But when his young friend Sam, left behind in New York, begins to suspect the "golden agers" are being mistreated, the news reaches Alex Kane's financier. Kane jumps into action, gaining the support of a local cowboy plucked right out of the Old West. These evil doers won't know what hit them when Alex Kane and his Cowboy ride into town!

"Preston's theme in these works is literature's most enduring: the conflict of good and evil – this time with homosexuals being the good guys."
— Jane D. Troxell

"If a book can be judged by how quickly you turn the pages, *Sweet Dreams* is a winner." — *Washington Blade*

A celebrated series of superhero adventure stories written for a general audience by bad boy John Preston whose journalism and fictional writings brought leather and bondage scene mainstream. This new edition includes a foreword by Philip Gambone (*As Far As I Can Tell: Finding My Father In World War II*).

Let's Get Criminal
Lev Raphael

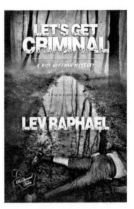

A Nick Hoffman / Academic Mystery, Book 1 – Nick Hoffman has everything he has ever wanted: a good teaching job, a nice house, and a solid relationship with his lover, Stefan Borowski, a brilliant novelist at the State University of Michigan. But when Perry Cross shows up, Nick's peace of mind is shattered. Not only does he have to share his office with the nefarious Perry, who managed to weasel his way into a tenured position without the right qualifications, he also discovers that Perry played a destructive role in Stefan's past. When Perry turns up dead, Nick wonders if Stefan might be involved, while the campus police force is wondering the same about Nick.

> "*Let's Get Criminal* is a delightful romp in the wonderfully petty and backbiting world of academia. Well-drawn characters make up a delicious list of suspects and victims." — Faye Kellerman

> "Reading *Let's Get Criminal* is like sitting down for a good gossip with an old friend. Its instant intimacy and warmth provides clever and sheer fun." — Marissa Piesman

Originally published in 1996, the first book in the Nick Hoffman Academic Mystery series is now back in print. This edition contains a new foreword by the author.

And don't miss ...

The Edith Wharton Murders: When Nick is forced to invite two warring Wharton societies to a SUM conference the conflict between rival scholars escalates from mudslinging to murder.

The Death of a Constant Lover: The son of a professor is murdered on a campus bridge and Nick's presence puts him in the middle of trouble.

Little Miss Evil: When cryptic messages in Nick's mailbox escalate into another corpse on campus, the reluctant sleuth is back on the case.

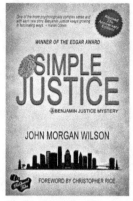

Simple Justice
John Morgan Wilson

A Benjamin Justice Mystery, Book 1 – It's 1994, an election year when violent crime is rampant, voters want action, and politicians smell blood. When a Latino teenager confesses to the murder of a pretty-boy cokehead outside a gay bar in L.A., the cops consider the case closed. But Benjamin Justice, a disgraced former reporter for the Los Angeles Times, sees something in the jailed boy others don't. His former editor, Harry Brofsky, now toiling at the rival Los Angeles Sun, surprises Justice from his alcoholic seclusion to help neophyte reporter Alexandra Templeton dig deeper into the story. But why would a seemingly decent kid confess to a brutal gang initiation killing if he wasn't guilty? And how can Benjamin Justice possibly be trusted, given his central role in the Pulitzer scandal that destroyed his career?

Snaking his way through shadowy neighborhoods and dubious suspects, he's increasingly haunted by memories of his lover Jacques, whose death from AIDS six years earlier precipitated his fall from grace. As he unravels emotionally, Templeton attempts to solve the riddle of his dark past and ward off another meltdown as they race against a critical deadline to uncover and publish the truth.

> "Wilson keeps the emotional as well as forensic suspense up through the very last sentence. The final scene is not only a satisfying explanation of the crime, but a riveting study of the erotic cruelty of justice." — *The Harvard Gay and Lesbian Review*

Awarded an Edgar by Mystery Writers of America for Best First Novel on initial release, this 25th Anniversary edition has been revised by the author. A foreword for the 2020 edition by Christopher Rice (*Bone Music*) is included.

Murder and Mayhem
Matt Lubbers-Moore

An Annotated Bibliography of Gay and Queer Males in Mystery, 1909-2018.

Librarian and scholar Matt Lubbers-Moore collects and examines every mystery novel to include a gay or queer male in the English language starting with Arthur Conan Doyle's "The Man with the Watches". Authors, titles, dates published, publishers, book series, short blurbs, and a description of how involved the gay or queer male character is with the mystery are included for a full bibliographic background.

Murder and Mayhem will prove invaluable for mystery collectors, researchers, libraries, general readers, aficionados, bookstores, and devotees of LGBTQ studies. The bibliography is laid out in alphabetical order by author including the blurb and author notes, whether a hard boiled private eye, an amateur cozy, a suspenseful romance, or a police procedural. All subgenres within the mystery field are included: fantasy, science fiction, espionage, political intrigue, crime dramas, courtroom thrillers, and more with a definition guide of the subgenres for a better understanding of the genre as a whole.

A ReQueered Tales Original Publication.

RICHARD STEVENSON

Something Inside
Conversations with Gay Fiction
Writers
Philip Gambone

In the late-20th century, gay literature had earned a place at the British and American literary tables, spawning its own constellation of important writers and winning a dedicated audience. This collection of probing interviews represents an attempt to offer a group portrait of the most important gay fiction writers.

The extraordinary power of the interviews, originally set down from 1987 to 1997, brings to life the passionate intellect of several voices now stilled among them Joseph Hansen, Allen Barnett, John Preston and Paul Monette. Others such as Scott Heim, Brad Gooch, Lev Raphael, Alan Hollinghurst and Michael Lowanthal were just tasting fame, even notoriety and have gone on to richly deserved acclaim. Published near the height of mainstream accolades for gay fiction as a category, Edmund White, David Plante, Andrew Holleran, Michael Cunningham and Christopher Bram had already enjoyed wide readership and two decades of scrutiny and broad readership.

Many of the pieces are accompanied by portraits from Robert Giard who set out, with urgency during the mid-1980s AIDS crisis, to capture gay artists in their prime; these images make a unique and profound contribution to this collection.

"A rich collective portrait of some of the most important and interesting gay writers of the last three decades."
— *Montreal Mirror*

Philip Gambone, a wise and insightful questioner, draws out incredible detail, emotion and personality in a context which still makes for compelling reading thirty years on. The author includes a 2022 update welcoming new readers to this indispensable resource.

⚠

**If you enjoyed this book,
please help spread the word
by posting a short,
constructive review at
your favorite social media site
or book retailer.**

**We thank you, greatly,
for your support.**

And don't be shy! Contact us!

*For more information about current and future releases,
please contact us:*

E-mail: *requeeredtales@gmail.com*
Facebook (Like us!): www.facebook.com/ReQueeredTales
Twitter: @ReQueered
Instagram: www.instagram.com/requeered
Web: www.ReQueeredTales.com
Blog: www.ReQueeredTales.com/blog
Mailing list (Subscribe for latest news): https://bit.ly/RQTJoin

264

www.ingramcontent.com/pod-product-compliance
Lightning Source LLC
Chambersburg PA
CBHW030203200225
22256CB00024BA/347